VIA Folios 65

Crossing the Alps

Best wishes,
Helen Barolini

Crossing the Alps

a novel by

Helen Barolini

BORDIGHERA PRESS

Library of Congress Control Number: 2010906731

Printed in the United States.

Published by
BORDIGHERA PRESS
John D. Calandra Italian American Institute
25 West 43rd Street, 17th Floor
New York, NY 10036

VIA FOLIOS 65
ISBN 978-1-59954-017-7

Table of Contents

Part One

Part Two

Part Three

Part One

Leaving

f rances Molletone was not "going to the Sorbonne" as appeared in the social column of the evening paper, an item called in by her mother.

She was going to Italy.

Which aroused a hostility and derision in her family that, two years before, a trip to Mexico had not and attendance at something as neutral as the Sorbonne would not. For Chrissake, her father said, what good will that do you, what future is there in Italy? Unspoken was the real question: why are you regressing? hadn't grandparents on both sides immigrated from Italy just so that she would have the opportunity to live, study, work, think, marry, breed American?

The war, in which Italy had been the enemy, was not long over. It was the summer of 1948 in upstate New York.

Fran tried to keep remote from the fracas (even as she translated it to *fracasso* in tribute to the Italian she was acquiring from Mr. di Tomasi). What was Italy to her except where Walter was?

Fran was used to her father's usual angry rejection of the old country which was occasionally broken by a proud recital of names: Dante, Michelangelo, Columbus, Marconi, when he was feeling boastful of his heritage compared to those like Poles or Irish who, he said, had nothing to show for themselves.

The night Fran made her announcement Frank Molletone rattled his evening paper irritably. Across the room from him stood the baby grand piano, untuned and unplayable, purchased by his wife Jenny to fill an awkward corner and provide display space for flowers and framed family photos. Above it was his portrait.

The unity of the cold portrait and untuned piano spoke bleak truths to Fran in the well furnished room. Fran felt insubstantial, of no importance in that house, nostalgic, in fact, for some other imagined home. What, besides her feeling of estrangement, did she know? -the beloved fairy tale books of her childhood; distrust of the Church into which she had been born but in which she put no faith; the joy of skiing, the beauty of Latin, the poetry of T.S. Eliot.

She also knew that she hovered over newness; that she wanted to find her place in the world; that she wanted love—that she would do anything—cross the Alps!—to get it.

That meant Walter. It no longer mattered to her that he was married. Once it had.

She's in the kitchen with her mother doing dishes. It's not long after she first met Walter Bongalli, the Italian post-graduate student in Forestry who was selected by the Rotary Club from among the University's foreign students to have Thanksgiving dinner with the Molletone family. Fran begins to cry as she stands near the sink.

Jenny Molletone looks up from washing the dishes. "What's wrong?"

"I didn't know," Fran stammers, pulling out choked words, struggling to say them. "He's married."

"You mean the Italian with that name? how does he say it, Valtair? So what? You didn't think you were going to marry him, did you?"

Her mother's turned back and abrupt words stifle Fran. She holds back the sobs and tries to breathe as she recovers impassivity. "No," she says lying. "It was just such a surprise. I wouldn't have gone out with him.... I didn't know how to deal with it."

"You've never known how to have the right boyfriends—but your father should have found out about him before inviting a foreigner here. Still, I suppose it was better than your not going out at all."

Even in her hurt, Fran partially understands that envy keeps her mother's back turned on her—envy that Fran is out in the world earning her own money, traveling, doing things Jenny Molletone has never done. Envy, maybe, that Fran feels love strongly enough to cry over it.

Fran recovers her composure. Hiding her feelings is just another disguise to add to those she has absorbed from childhood: since Italian is backward and scorned, be like her friends with the American names. Cultivate sang froid, the impassive face, not caring.

Home is where one starts from, says Eliot.

Jenny Molletone always recouped a bad situation with festivity. She gave parties. Liking appearances and reasons for getting out the silver, she gave what she called a bon voyage party for her daughter.

The guests were her women friends and some relatives, to one of whom, Lena Gugino, Fran was explaining that the paper had gotten it wrong about the Sorbonne; she would only be passing through Paris, then Switzerland, on her way to Italy.

"Italy! How come, Fran, wasn't it bombed?"

While Fran hesitated, wondering if Lena thought there was no more country, that the boot had upended and sunk out of sight into *mare nostrum*, a voice crashed into her forming reply.

"She's turning into a wop, that's why!"

It was Bunny Markee and her words broke in the midst of the party like an unforeseen summer shower, sudden and inciting. Whenever Fran heard Bunny's absurd name, she felt the tension. 'Bunny' was a nickname for the full-blown Maria Abbondanza of her baptism, and the re-doing of Marchi into 'Markee' was the concession made a priori to those who would mispronounce the name Marchee. Also present in the room were the other concessionaires: Mrs. Yennock whose name was americanized from Iannocchio; Mrs. Cianci who mispronounced her name See'n-see since she didn't want to seem "Chanchy", and Ginny Gagliardi who let herself be called Gag-lee-ard-eye.

Mr. di Tomasi had the greatest contempt for these corruptions: "Names are our sign that we own ourselves," he told Fran. At their first lesson he corrected her mispronouncing her name Molle-tone-, and guided her to Mo-leh-toney. If Americans can say lasagna and Pagliacci, he told her, they can say your name correctly and any name. It's up to everyone to guide them and not let them have the last say. If you lose your name, everything else goes.

Fran wanted to agree but she had known, as Mr. di Tomasi had not, the anxiety of introductions at sorority rushes when some Sally Smith would look at her name-tag and say, Now that's interesting, how do you say it? And Fran would say her name, only to have it repeated mangled, and finally given up in a sputter of giggles and eye-rolling, marking her as strange in that covey of All-American girls. Fran had gone through the rushing to show she was someone, not just her name, sure she'd succeed and that once accepted she'd never have anything to fear again.

But she wasn't accepted. At some houses she had been told they only accepted one or two Catholics a year, and she had never told them she was no longer a Catholic for it was a personal matter that had been painful for her to go through and was not yet resolved, and then it might seem as if she were saying that just to get in; no one said what the policy was for those who compounded the handicap of being Catholic with that of having an Italian name. Maybe no such creature had been seen in rushing before.

To Mr. di Tomasi's scorn for name-changers, Fran had no answer except to wonder if it might not be better to change yourself from Iannocchio to Yennock before the others did it to you.

Bunny's voice, always too loud and coarse and identifiable with the Italian West side which Fran loathed, was hard with accusation. Her pig-eyes were sunk in a flaccid face while her lips, huge red slashes, curled as she spoke. She blew cigarette smoke from her nostrils. Behind her back she was known as Misery Markee for her stinginess.

Bunny was second cousin to Frank Molletone. A short-legged, square woman in her early forties who had worked in Frank's office before she married, she looked to Fran like an overweight version of one of the Andrews sisters in a beige suit which strained across her thick middle and from which a turquoise blouse ruffled at her neckline. Her amber-blonde hair, of which she was conspicuously proud, was rolled back at the sides in thick sausages ending in a pompadour that jutted out over her forehead like an entablature.

Fran's hair was reddish brown, worn long and loose and up-turned slightly from her forehead. Her face was full and fair; her gray-green eyes were set off by well-defined, arched brows, her mouth usually set in a close-lipped smile. A chipped front tooth made her self-conscious and kept her from smiling broadly, giving her a dreamy, artless look as if detached from what was going on.

Fran liked fashionable clothes and wore the New Look that Dior had just introduced to signal the end of wartime restrictions on fabric and style—a full-skirted, almost ankle-length blue and green sleeveless dress of impressionistic window-pane design topped by a wasp-waisted lime-green jacket She felt light years ahead of everybody there.

Bunny was standing, cigarette between two fingers of one hand, a Minton cup and saucer in the other hand, at the dining room table, which Jenny Molletone had set with her best linen and silver tea service. In the center was a floral arrangement of pink and white carnations set off by green laurel. It might have been a bridal shower. It should have been, Fran could hear the unspoken thoughts of the women in the room, sorry for their friend Jenny.

Fran felt separate from the room, and from the fine house, which gave her no answers to who she really was but merely told her who she could pretend to be. It had been meant to excise all that shadowy part which now emerged in Bunny's words.

Wop. Reject. Part of some lower order. The word created such dissonance in the fine house, awakening echoes everyone wanted stilled, that Fran fancied she could hear the rattling of the English bone-china in the corner cabinet. It was a word that chilled every-one, wrapping them in a collective taint and allying them with a late-arrived, very dark Sicilian cousin who was so backward she still kept animals in her yard to slaughter on feast days. This dark relative, however, had a daughter who had married Irish and with her new name had, as Jenny Molletone concluded the telling, "gotten away from all the stigma".

Wop! Was that Walter? Mr. di Tomasi?

Fran thought of Thanksgiving when, in the person of Walter, being Italian had begun to be something attractive. She had silently studied him across a table decorated with cornucopia and chrysanthemums. He had a lean, sharp look and a biting tone that was at odds with the other guests, two well-mannered South Americans who were cadets at a nearby military academy. The Italian was already a *dottore* from an Italian university and was saying things in a sharp, ironic, often bitterly humorous way—a way no American, or cadet, spoke. Walter related in good English his experience during the war as an interpreter for British troops pushing up to Florence through the Gothic Line.

It was strange, Fran thought, that at a dinner celebrating excess with such native things as crammed turkey gigantica, creamed corn, hubbard squash and pumpkin pie, and across from parents who would have been startled to know it, the elegance of the Roman elegiac poets hit her as it had not in the Latin seminars that her father's railroad-cars of bananas and literal lettuce had paid for. The war had been good to Frank Molletone. People always had to eat. And it rewarded him to have at his table someone from defeated Italy to see how well he had done.

When Fran went out with him, Walter had been critical of her not knowing Italian.

"I've studied French and Spanish," she told him. He was not impressed.

"Your language should have been Italian," he said sternly. "It's the language of your people."

Well, no, she had silently corrected, thinking of the grandparents with whom she had never been able to speak; what they spoke was not Italian but the harsh sounding dialect of the far-off regions in the bottom of the boot they had come from.

"I've had Latin, so it shouldn't be so hard to learn," Fran told Walter.

"Try this." He handed her a copy of his *Gazzetta*, a weekly Italian language paper full of the words and feelings and expressions that no one in her family had thought it worthwhile giving her.

Shortly after, she went to *La Gazzetta's* offices to place an ad for an Italian tutor. She had lived all her life in her city without knowing that the *Gazzetta* existed; it was a lowly, struggling paper filled with pictures of First Communions and the social events of people she wanted nothing to do with. In the *Gazzetta* office she found Mr. di Tomasi, editor, administrator, typesetter for the paper, who, instead of taking her ad, offered himself to teach her Italian in his home.

He was a soft-spoken man, with a patience that Fran learned spoke more of substance and strength than resignation. His shoulders sloped from curving over type for hours; his eyes were mild and gray behind the glasses that were the badge of his profession. He had come to America in the late 1920's from the hard, mountainous, central part of Italy called the Abruzzi. He was not an illiterate laborer driven by poverty, but an idealist out of sympathy with the fascist regime.

He was genuinely pleased that Fran wanted to learn Italian. He would give her lessons in his home each evening after supper, he said. He wanted no payment. And Fran thought of all the fine things she would send him from Italy when she got there including copies of Italian newspapers and magazines because he had told her confidentially that, yes, *La Gazzetta* was really the *porcheria* everyone said it was. He couldn't, working alone, catch all the errors. But as bad as it was, it kept something alive among the people on the North side. When it was gone, so was their language.

Fran went to Mr. di Tomasi's home each night in the old Chevy her father had let her have to get to the University. They sat in a clean white kitchen which showed not a sign of the supper he and his wife and children had just eaten. At the kitchen table Fran spent the months following Walter's return to Italy, conjugating verbs, learning the impure "s" and the polite form of address. By early summer she haltingly began to speak Walter's native language.

"*Ma perchè così straziarmi,*" she finally confronted him one night, the words perfectly pronounced and right out of a Rossini opera. "*Brava!*" he exclaimed, ignoring her protest for his plying her with difficult verbs. The phrase came fluently, liquidly from her lips. It was as if she had crossed some magic divide, as she never had with the other languages.

Fran said goodby to Mr. di Tomasi just before her mother's party. He was sad and stooped. They had begun to speak of many things including the harshness Italians had suffered in their own land and how they had had to immigrate, leaving with nothing, often not even a proper language to help them understand the world.

Fran was moved. She told him she would write to him in Italian and send him news of his country once she got there. He said, "My country is a poor and beautiful place. I do not hate her."

"And I never will!" Fran had rejoined with a just-born fervor.

But in her own home, hearing *wop!* and recoiling from it, Fran felt like another St. Peter denying Christ. Just by recoiling she denied Mr. di Tomasi and the beauty of the language he had given her, denied his generousness and his pride in his native country - denied everything except the sense of shame Bunny had hit in her.

The others laughed in a nervous tremolo as if they had been found out, their disguise penetrated. If Fran were a wop, why then they all were. Fran felt transformed to when she was nine or ten, a skinny kid at the downtown YWCA filling in the membership form and pausing at the blank for nationality. She was uncertain of what to put: was she American because of being born there, or was she Italian because that's what her name was and that's what everyone said she was. Timidly, she voiced her dilemma to the woman at the desk: and when, after some questioning, she was told peremptorily, why you're American, of course!, she still wasn't persuaded.

To name is to know: her name marked her just as much as black skin or slanted eyes marked a person. It's how she was judged.

But what if she weren't Frances Molletone? What if, like a lobotomy that could change personality, she were changed to Fran Miller? -like Daisy, Maud, Henry and Glenn. She'd be a different person immediately. In fact, for the first time she'd *be* a person in her own right, not just a caricature defined by her name. How her life might have advanced!

"Come on, Bunny, she's got talent!" Lena Gugino's retort rang in the air, putting Fran back into the party scene.

"Give the kid credit," Lena was saying. "If you had the brains, and had gone to college, you'd be doing the same thing!"

"Not me," said Bunny. "I'm an American -I'm not going back to being no wop!"

What, Fran wondered, made Bunny Markee so angry about Italy? Wasn't it America she was really angry at? It was America, after all, who made them wops. Bunny was dragging hard on her cigarette, provocative and challenging.

"She's always been different, Bunny," said Jenny Molletone. The look and tone of betrayal left Fran in no doubt that her mother felt cheated in her only daughter.

Emotions were rife in the air with Bunny's raid on the party. This was not an English tea-party but war between peasant women at the village well. One of them was going beyond the village walls. It threatened them all. It meant dishonor to the parents with whom a female should be housed until marriage took her from the patriarchal home to the husband's; it meant defiance to the code that said a single woman had no business going out in the world on her own; it meant an upset in values—how could the women who stayed behind be content with their lot if one left?

The signs of warning had been posted: "The most important thing you can learn is not in college, it's how to make your parents happy." Or, "Nothing can replace family; blood is thicker than water."

Despite which, Fran had always known that someday she would leave them all behind; it was in the books she lugged home from the library when she used to stop there every Saturday after confession at Holy Name church, it was in her thoughts, in the diary she kept, in the Latin poets like Lucretius she had read in college, in her restlessness, and in the visceral homesickness for someplace else with which she seemed to have been born.

Fran felt the currents and the electricity in the room. The women were as wound-up as coiled springs. So long as routine and observance of tradition kept them steady, they had strength in their tenacity, in knowing how to manipulate, in becoming skillful in backbiting; but let something unhinge the restraints they had always lived with, and they uncoiled violently. Fran's stepping out of line had done it.

She would sail to France, third class on an old pre-war Dutch relic left over from better days. She would stay with a college classmate in Paris who actually was studying at the Sorbonne, then she'd go on to Switzerland to visit someone else. France and Switzerland were incidental, handy to her plan to lead up to Italy gradually. Switzerland was the neutral point from which to cross barriers—Alps and others. It was symbol, it was decision and act, it was saying who she was to be. (But all that she would know later.)

For the moment it was enough for Fran that she wanted to be in Italy to meet up again with an Italian who had gone home.

Part Two

Rome

On the February night when Frances Molletone got off the 106 tram in Rome at Piazza Fiume, it was not yet tourist Rome. She could feel herself, as an American, rather alone and strange in the city. She was aware of the difference, because the Italians made her so the moment she began speaking their language: "*Americana?*" the newspaper vendor or the barman serving her cappuccino or the person from whom she got directions asked. They were like curious children, quite unselfconscious of being intrusive, eager to find out what she, an American, was doing here? Did she like Rome? Did she find it beautiful? Fran liked this singling out, this seeing herself in a new way.

It was cold that February night in Rome. Fran huddled deeper into her coat -so green and square-cut and collegiate, so out of place for Rome, for Italy- and crossed the street. Even as she looked about the opposite corner for the person she was to meet, she saw him, the professor, in his black overcoat and hat. There was a book tucked under his arm as there always was when he walked into the large, shadowy room of the palazzo where he gave lessons in Italian to a few resident foreigners of whom Fran was one. He walked with clipped, sure step toward her and when they met, he tipped his hat and said good evening.

Fran smiled in greeting and wondered if this formal, rather short, middle-aged Italian professor who had invited her to see St.

Peter's with him by night were always what the dark garb, the tucked book and trim walk indicated. What did it matter if he were? Nothing, she decided, nothing at all. It was just another night to pass and just as well he had brought a book along.

"Do you mind, *signorina*, if we take the streetcar?" Even as he asked, Professor Balestrini was guiding her toward the stop for the *circolare rossa*, the streetcar that circled the heart of Rome completely and continuously on every forty-five minute trip.

"I love the *circolare*," Fran smiled.

Gregorio Balestrini recognized that what she said so unselfconsciously was true. Americans, in their constant wonder at things, loved everything; their enthusiasms were limitless. Streetcars, culture, food and drink, classical ruins, movie stars, royalty, democracy —it was all the same to them. He did not know any other Americans than this Miss Molletone, and she only from his classroom, but he read their literature. He was willing to put up with a crowded, dirty, jolting streetcar because it was cheap and available, but he would never love it as this American girl did.

Balestrini scanned her to see if there were, as certainly with an Italian, an undercurrent of irony in her words. But no; she was artless. She was pretty, very pretty. And serene. Had it been otherwise, Balestrini asked himself, would he have gone out on a cold night if the girl weren't at least pretty? But that was all she was. She had nothing of the bold femaleness of Italian women, pretty or not.

Frances Molletone wore a beret, low shoes with an ankle strap like a child's, and a large leather bag was slung over her shoulder. If she had been ironic, her outfit would have seemed an act of self-parodying waifishness. Balestrini thought of how a woman of Rome would have gotten herself up for an evening appointment. Again he told himself to remember about American girls: she has an Italian name but she's as American as an Isabel Archer, a Daisy Miller... ingenuous, without the inner sense which makes her European counterpart so aware of herself as woman. It was the novelty of Miss Molletone, more than anything else, that appealed to him. The other women in his class were secretaries or Embassy wives, British and Austrian mostly, European at any rate and not attractive to him.

"What a bargain the *circolare* is," she was saying. "Only ten lire a ride and there's no end of the line where the conductor calls out *il viaggio è terminato* as they do on the other lines. The first time I got on a *circolare* it was by mistake, but I stayed and made the whole round trip. It was wonderful—you can see the best of Rome in an hour."

"Or even spend the night aboard if you're poor and have no other place to sleep," he returned her smile.

He was pleasant, but his look and words had an edge that made Fran uncertain and she became silent. She thought of the old, odorous streetcars, which jerked and lurched in their perpetual circuit of Rome.

Because it was so cheap to ride and always kept going, night and day, the *circolare* was always crowded and if she loved it, Fran had to admit, it was when she had managed to find a seat or stand in the very back to look out the window as they hurtled past the old wall near Porta Pinciana, past the busy piazza at Porta Pia, past the railroad station, past the basilica of Santa Maria Maggiore, the Coliseum, the Circus Maximus, the island in the Tiber, Castel Sant' Angelo, the Ministry of Justice, until the streetcar clanked its way up the avenue of the Tortuous Wall at the edge of Villa Borghese and back to Porta Pinciana. There was something distinctly Roman about the *circolare*—its oldness, its crowdedness, its discomfort, its interminability, and its humanity—that appealed to Fran as much as the city it circled. Whenever the exchange rate for her dollars rose or fell on the black market, she re-figured her ride in pennies; now it was not quite a penny and a half. As the streetcar rumbled to their stop, Fran pulled ten lire from her coat pocket.

"Please, please," said the professor firmly as he motioned her to put away her money. Squeezed among the people on the platform, Fran watched him get two tickets from the unshaven ticketman. And because the sight of the formal professor in the midst of all the shoving, scowling, smelly passengers was so incongruous and somehow touching, she said for his sake, "I think most people who ride this streetcar must come off misanthropes."

"Not at all!" he exclaimed, to her surprise. "It is just a question of equilibrium with the feet and with the mind. You don't have to love it or hate it—only to balance yourself." Seeing her wedged among the swaying forms in the aisle, he asked with concern, "Are you uncomfortable?"

"*No, no, sto bene.*"

Because they were packed so tightly in the car and so many arms, stretched to the handrail above, latticed the space between Frances and the professor, it was hard to keep talking and they fell silent. They were so unknown to each other that their silence was as natural as if they were strangers and neither felt compelled to talk. This made the trolley trip and the prospect of the evening easier, not as unusual as it first seemed to Fran.

The streetcar shook its way along desperately and though she couldn't see, Fran thought they must be going through Villa Borghese and squirmed a bit to look out. All she managed was a closer view of the professor, three-quarter profile under the black hat. He was blondish, his eyes almost blue, and his face was square with taut, scarred skin. He didn't look Italian as she had thought of them at home. Now she could distinguish those of the north. They were beyond Piazza Flaminia when it occurred to Fran that the professor reminded her of Professor Nunn at the university. This amused her. How could she have imagined, not even two years ago, when she was still in college and intimidated by professors that she'd be riding in a Rome streetcar with one who wanted to explain the Baroque to her? Never, she decided, could it have happened with Mr. Nunn, her English teacher. Impossible with someone named Wilfred Nunn. Impulsively Fran turned to the professor and said, "Excuse me, *professore*, but what is your first name?"

Amused, Balestrini answered quietly over his shoulder, "Gregorio."

Good, she thought. She liked the hard "r's" combined with the rolling vowels. It was strong, like Walter, not as mellifluous as some Italian names for men.

"And you, signorina?"

"Francesca." She liked her name in Italian. Although the professor knew English, they had been speaking Italian, using, as in class, the polite third person form of address. The streetcar rattled over a bridge and crossed the Tiber and Fran mused about Professor Nunn of the prudent name and this professor of the formal grammar. And she herself: Fran of east coast America, now well out of there and pleased with the evening. She decided it would sound well in Italian and said to Balestrini, "*È molto suggestiva questa gita sulla circolare, e questa serata.*" He smiled.

She had, at first, been perplexed at this idea of his. He was so austere in class, so remote from anything but relentless pronunciation drills and insistence on the most obscure grammatical rules. Then one evening after the lesson he left the classroom when she did instead of lingering in the chill room to answer questions or wait for the janitor. They had walked together to the tram stop where they found, with surprise, that they took the same number tram and actually lived not far from each other. They had spoken in vague, polite terms and he continued to correct her grammar. Tell me, he had asked on the tram, do you like Rome? What do you think of its Baroque architecture?

She said, of course she loved Rome, but she preferred the classical to the Baroque, which seemed to her redundant, too billowy, too full of flourishes.

But that, he had rejoined strongly, is why it's so civilized. The expression of civilization *is* redundancy and superfluousness. Baroque is a highest expression of style and Rome, despite its apparent conglomeration, is the most civilized of cities because it's so triumphantly baroque.

Take St. Peter's, he exclaimed, there's nothing else like it!—it's the culmination of the baroque spirit. And he asked her if she had seen it at night, to which she replied no.

Then we shall go this Friday evening, he had said.

And because he had been so very serious and decided, Fran had agreed. She thought that St. Peter's would be improved by night when there were no rosary sellers or visitors about. And later she realized something more: although the days she spent walking through Rome weren't difficult, the nights spent alone in her room were.

When the streetcar approached Ponte Sant'Angelo, Balestrini took Fran by the arm and said, "We get off here."

There on the bridge of angels his correct, professorial air left him and he became a man enthralled. "Look!" he exclaimed, stopping and pointing to the huge white marble sculptures that overlooked the walkway, "look down this bridge! Here's Bernini—look at the movement in each of his angels—look at the way they move, each differently. You can feel the motion increase as you walk past!" He became excited by his words. He was not much taller than Fran, but as he expressed his thoughts he stretched his neck and lifted his head upward as if a visible increase in height would increase his authority.

Fran looked at the angels that lined the bridge at intervals on either side and bore, each one, a different instrument of Christ's agony. They were large, round-faced angels with legs in semblance of swirling movement, unpinioned wings, cloud-drift backgrounds, all in a rich plasticity of motion.

"But they are too... too matronly," Fran said.

Balestrini stopped in annoyance and shook his head. "You can't understand anything until you understand that this is the most beautiful bridge in the world!"

"More beautiful than Pont Neuf?" she murmured, having not long before seen it in Paris.

"Yes, yes," he said impatiently. "Pont Neuf is sterile, it hasn't the movement, the flamboyance, the daring of this. Look! *Magnifico!*"

Balestrini's excitement reached her and as she looked down the length of the bridge, Fran began to see the drama of the big, awkward angels. They gleamed white along the parapet and stood in bright relief from the dark huddled mass of old Castel Sant'Angelo on whose pagan summit a vengeful St. Michael stood, raising his sword against the night. Above, the clouds were torn across the sky as if they had been first stretched taut, then snapped, and left hanging with straggling edges. There was not a sound, not a person.

"How distant the moon is tonight," Fran said as if to herself.

She felt moved by the light which shone from the statues and seemed to hold the whole bridge, with them on it, in suspension from the surrounding dark. She glanced at the man at her side. He was watching her. He was calm once more, correct and contained. He took her arm and they started up long, still Via della Conciliazione leading to St. Peter's.

Balestrini felt unsure about the prospects of the evening; the American obviously lacked the deep culture upon which his words could resonate properly. She was raw, sharp, angular, and he felt his ideas tearing to shreds upon her jagged Americaness. On the other hand, her freshness moved him. He had long had it in mind to spend an evening with *signorina* Molletone.

"Ah,... it is a night, really a night," he almost chanted.

Yes, she thought, not like all the others. As they entered the great square of St. Peter's, she was glad she had come. The colonnades of the piazza circled them like giant lobster claws, the four-deep columns of such perfect formation that they appeared to be one. Two great fountains on either side of a thrusting obelisk spilled ecstatically into great round basins, delighting Fran that such a perfect phallic formation stood at the heart of Christendom. Set into the pavement around the obelisk was the compass of the winds with their evocative names: *ponente maestro, tramontana, scirocco, greco levante....*

Balestrini led her to the shadowed portico and they sat at the base of a column, looking up obliquely at the basilica's façade as the professor's hands shaped themselves in that direction and he spoke to her of the massiveness, the grandeur, the colossal and subtle complexity of St. Peter's. Even as Fran looked where he pointed at the line of apostles along the pediment, she thought they lacked the drama of the obelisk right there under the Pope's nose.

But that was Rome. A mix of everything. What had she read in her Latin classes? -*Homo sum, humani nihil a me alienum puto.* I am human, nothing human can be alien to me. Nothing was strange and contradictory in Rome. Not even the fact that she was there.

Each day that passed Rome became more seductive. The upheaval of the city felt right—the classic ruins crusted over with Renaissance, festooned with Baroque, squared with the modernism of the Fascist regime. She had stood in the debris of the great Forum and related the fallen chunks of columns, architraves and pediments to herself after finding an entry in Hawthorne's Rome diary that described the sights of Rome as "crumbs of various ruin dropped from the devouring maw of time." How apt! how perfect for Fran whose mother's maiden name was Briciola, "crumb." There she was, crumb of a long line of crumbs in the one place on earth where she could be at home among the variegate crumbs of time.

Only in that milennial capital that had witnessed everything could she come to terms with her feelings of love and loneliness. They became bearable when she walked down a street and came, say, to the delight of the turtle fountain with its joy of life and its mandate to be nothing more than pleasurable; or the portico of Octavia and adjacent alleys where stumps of classical columns emerged from walls. Sometimes she sat on a low wall and seemed to watch all the cats of Rome sun themselves along the ancient back-side of the Pantheon. The long reach of time past was a soothing unguent to the heat of time present. And the people helped. They were handsome, elegant, flippant, brittle and unsentimental; and she saw in them the same cunning expressions she viewed in the museum busts of their ancestors. Intact in them was the vitality that survived the city's various eclipses. Passed in the street, the Romans looked their part—cosmopolitan chameleons. In such a place she was no outsider, her name no burden.

As a silver bell tonged against the cold edge of the night and sounded a quarter-hour, the professor took the book from under his arm and said, "I shall read Baudelaire to you."

His carefully modulated voice took on warmer tones and when the hour was sounded by a deep bronze bell, Fran could feel the change just as she felt the timbre of the bronze in contrast to the silver. He began to express the same current of excitement as on the bridge. Fran, with her eyes on the façade, began to see the images of the verse: young girls of Lesbos stroking with sterile voluptuousness the ripe fruit of their own bodies; trembling fingers plunged into thick locks; undulant forms, the lush body of a tawny creole, the strong smell of musk, blood-filtered light, carrion, death, the cry *'Je te hais autant que je t'aime!'* reminding her of Walter and the line from Catullus, *Odi et amo*, that she inscribed in her books.

All through the reading, through the silver bells and the second booming of the bronze, Fran sat with her back against a column and regarded St. Peter's. Beautiful, she thought, but too ripe... both Baudelaire and St. Peter's. Baroque was a great stew of Mediterranean emotion, a whiff of heavy summer when colors, noises, odors are intensified and make one fatigued.

"Oh, to be in England, now that April's there," Fran murmured softly.

Balestrini looked up from his book his eyebrows raised in surprise. "Browning? Are you tired?"

"Yes," she said, "it's late." But more than tired she felt what the professor had conjured into the night like a ripe decadence hanging over them. This was the lure, she thought, this carefully planned nightscape in baroque.

As if taken by a sudden chill she hunched into her coat, shivering. Balestrini reached for her hands and rubbed them quickly in his to warm her. His face was animated as he said, "You are Baudelaire's *beau navire—D'un air placide et triomphant, tu passes ton chemin, majestueuse enfant*. He is perfect."

"He is sick," Fran said sulkily.

Balestrini laughed in delight, then looked surprised as she pulled her hands away from his and put them into her pockets. Now he was getting silly; she wanted in some way to retaliate. "All those sick images," she said in a rush, "it's..." and as she searched for words she looked towards the apostles lining the pediment of the great basilica. Balestrini watched her fascinated. "It's impotence disguised!" she finished.

A sound of footsteps clacked through the long colonnade and a seminarian in black robes and a purple sash came out of the shadows and passed by, his head lowered.

"Speaking of impotence," Balestrini chuckled. Rising, he extended his hand to Fran and said, "Shall we leave?"

Coming into the piazza, Fran pointed to a light in a Vatican window." The Pope is praying to cover the sound of Baudelaire which you raised," she said with a smile, calm again, detached.

"He will be praying for Cardinal Mindszenty, imprisoned by the communists," Balestrini answered, his manner once more formal, professorial.

"Then he shouldn't have such pagan fountains to drown out the sound of his prayers."

They went into one of the many bars along the Via della Conciliazione and sat at a little marble-topped table in the empty place. They had cognac in *caffè espresso* and the drink warmed and eased Fran. "I have enjoyed tonight," she said.

"Truly? Good! then we can do it again," Balestrini said politely. He was guarded. There was something confusing in this American, something he could not get at.

"Yes, let's," said Fran, looking him in the eye. "How about Catullus in the Coliseum?—it could be even better."

"You're not afraid to end up like your countrywoman Daisy Miller?" he teased. He was curious about her, about her presence in his class, where she presented the dreamy moon-face of a peasant Madonna; either she was bland, or cagily inscrutable. But the evening had disclosed a vein of tension in her. She was not all what she first suggested.

"What do you do here in Rome, *signorina* Francesca?"

"I go to your classes."

"Only that?"

"I walk through the city... I write poetry... I sketch... I look around and pass the time."

"Why do you come to my classes?"

"I must have my visa renewed. I can stay as long as I'm a student."

"But the classes will end soon. Not enough people attend to make them worthwhile."

Fran looked dismayed. "They'll end? Then what can I do?"

"To carry on your Italian, you mean?"

"No. To stay. Here, in Rome."

He regarded her with interest. She spoke with such emphasis that to him, Italian, it could mean only one thing. "You have someone here you want to be near?"

Fran's expression didn't change as she returned his look and nodded silently. But she thought to herself that any other teacher she had known, like Professor Nunn and the others, would have asked if there were *something*, not someone, she wanted to stay for, like a research project, art studies, travels. Balestrini had guessed right and Fran was impressed by that.

"Don't worry," he said, "you may petition to stay to continue your studies, I will sign it for you." He was relieved to know this of her for it explained her strangeness and vague absent air. Complications did not discourage him. *Anzi!* he told himself. Just as fire feeds fire, so obstacles feed an attraction.

"But what about the classes?"

"At my home, if you wish."

But this was not her humble tutor back home, Fran told herself as she weighed Balestrini's words. There'd be no meeting in the parlor to do verbs with an affable wife in the background. Already Fran knew something of Italian men, their separate lives, the non-accessibility of their homes and families to outsiders. Balestrini was spoofing.

"I can't disturb your family," she said.

"In the Colosseum, then."

She smiled and shook her head. Let him have his joke, she thought. Silently they left the bar and walked the empty street. "We can get a tram from here," Balestrini said, "it will be less crowded than the *circolare.*"

The tram was almost deserted. Fran headed for seats but Balestrini took her arm and said, "Let's stay back here—we can look out at the city."

She leaned against a rail in the back corner and looked out at the city lights while the professor got their tickets. Returning, he stood directly before her, one arm braced straight against the window behind her head and the other at the rail by her side so that, despite all the room on the back platform, she was hemmed in by what was, actually, his embrace. They talked softly of the city they passed through. Each time they swayed with the motion of the tram she was thrown towards him. He took his arm from the window and put it around her shoulder and with the other unbuttoned her coat. Fran stared amazed at the professor who still spoke to her in the formal third person. He answered her look saying in a low voice, the voice she had heard in the colonnade, "I have wanted to for a long time."

Foolishly, Fran could only say, "But the conductor!"

"I have paid for the tickets." One hand was inside her coat and the other held her head as he leaned forward to kiss her. She slapped him. He drew back, releasing her.

"*Che barbara!*" he exclaimed. Then, laughing ruefully, "You are very rude, *signorina*."

"Let's walk," she said, "it's not far from here." Did the professor think she had meant *him* when she said there was someone in Rome she wanted to stay for?

Outside Balestrini took her arm and asked, exactly as she expected him to, "You do not like me?"

Fran knew that it would be taken as another breach of manners to suggest that he did not excite her if, as had happened, he had tried. She did not want to offend Balestrini or hurt his pride by saying she not think of him in those terms. So she said with a veil of implied regret, "But you have a wife. I have a friend in Rome. There is nothing to do."

Balestrini looked up at the distant moon in the dark, starless sky. The chill wind of the *tramontana* blew about them. "And is it not possible I still feel something for you?"

These weeks in Rome, and the months before at home, Fran's resolve had been as straight and firm as a Roman column, a monument of sorts to Walter. Now for no good reason she felt the monument buckle; it was as if an imperceptible hairline crack began to widen and fan out. She felt the pressure of some undetected but present inner stress. And what did it say of her love for Walter?—a love premised on its having no chance. She had thought she was strong, and now she realized she was also lonely. But she answered Balestrini calmly, "No, it is not possible."

"And your lover, where is he while you are here with me?"

It was the first time anyone had ever spoken to her of a lover. Was Walter her lover? Not as Balestrini indubitably meant; but he was the one she loved, the reason she was there. He was more, not less, than a lover but this would be too difficult to explain to the professor.

"He's married," she said.

"Ah!" Balestrini's face lit up and he laughed softly as he said, almost to himself, "He does not make love to you—you meet him by day, and quite seldom."

"Yes," said Fran, ashamed.

"But my dear, *è impossibile!* You are young and warm, you *want* to be loved. And you are in the hands of this jester who will keep you waiting until he is ready or can figure out how to manage it - someone who knows already you'll be his. He is your first love?"

"Yes."

"That is not good, not good at all. Especially if you love him! You are too trusting. He will toy with you, you will be hurt."

"No, *professore*, you are wrong." Her strangled words came hard past the knot in her throat. "You see, it is because he doesn't want to hurt me that he hasn't...."

"I am sorry, my dear, but *you* are wrong. It is because his wife still pleases him in bed and you are only a conceptualized adventure of some kind that he treats you like this. Now he only caresses you and speaks vaguely to you, but already you exaggerate his effect. He has appealed to your imagination and to your pride. When he does make love to you, you will be lost. Is he young?"

"Twenty-six."

"It will never last! He won't know how to keep up the romantic suspense, the play of imagination. He will become impatient as you become more and more insistent. You will start begging him for even small attentions. After your pride is gone, there can be no delight, only pain." Balestrini stopped and taking her by both hands, looked at her fondly. "You will lose a lot, *signorina.*"

Tears came to Fran's eyes. She wanted to protest, to tell the professor he was cynical and cruel, a man of cold, academic airs who had no understanding of what was between Walter and her. But she felt that he wasn't cruel, that he had merely put into words her own premonitions.

"But I love him!"

"Of course you do. Or you would not walk through Rome all day waiting to meet him, or come to my class for the dubious pleasure of conjugating verbs. But you will only love him best when you are free. Now you are not free."

"You're wrong," she cried, bewildered by what he was saying.

Balestrini tried to remember when he had been young enough and naive enough to be as moved as she was by love. He no longer believed in love; he believed in the demands of sex and the appeal of dalliances to hold at bay the knowledge of unhappiness and an unaccomplished life. But love? He raised his hands in a gesture of bewilderment: "But my young woman, what do you want? You have the courage to be here and at the same time the foolishness to smother everything with sentimentality! *Signorina*, you appreciate the nuances of love no better than you did the Baroque."

Fran lashed back, "You're wrong!" She rushed through the gate at the drive, past the porter's house and up to the building where she paused at the great outer door and looked angrily at the man in black. She was unhappy and troubled and he, still calm and smiling.

She said sharply, "Why aren't you happy with your wife?"

He shrugged his shoulders. "I am not really displeased. We married too young, I suppose, and passionate love gets spent, used up, just as everything does. All that is left, then, is a comfortable home arrangement—like a well-kept hotel, or one's private club. And now, when I feel myself stimulated and attracted by someone fresh I see no reason to deny pleasure." He was no longer laughing or using his hands to gesture. He was quiet again and serious and he looked directly at Fran as he did in class to ask her a question. For the first time he used the familiar form of address and she was touched by the gentle intimacy of it as he said, "You must see that I feel a great emotion for you."

She turned and opened the great door; he accompanied her into the hall where the ground floor apartments and elevator were. "Where do you stay?" he asked.

"Here," she said going to a door at the left side of the hall. "I have a room with a family." She unlocked the apartment door and turned to say goodnight. The professor had taken off his hat and without it he looked neither so formal, nor so self-assured. He looked a little old, a little sad. Fran did not dislike him.

Almost as if to ward off an evil augury, or a future presentiment, she said, "Would you like to come in?

Balestrini was in an entrance hall very much like that of his own apartment, like that of all Rome apartments of a certain age. Near the entrance, the same heavy-legged refectory table with telephone and pieces of mail that he saw everyday in his own hallway and, above the table, even the same type of art print—whether cows pasturing in the ruins of 18th century Rome, or a lady on a swing in a Boucher France, or the hunt in England. It was all the same. The same long, marble-floored corridor punctuated by closed doors on either side; the same stillness; the same sense of propriety and things never changing. Only one thing made this place different from his— Fran standing in her doorway motioning to him.

"We must be quiet," she said. "There's a Chinese student on one side of me, and two elderly English ladies on the other. They all go to bed early and hate to be disturbed."

"Certainly," Balestrini whispered. "And the head of the house, does he hate to be disturbed?"

"The family head is a widowed duchess. She and her children and the maid live down the hall in the back. I see the girls at mealtime and the duchess only to pay the rent. She has all her meals in her room and almost never goes out. She's rather young, too, and nice looking."

"And what is the name of this discrete duchess?" Balestrini asked in an offhand manner as he gazed about Fran's room.

"She's the Duchessa di Sant'Elpidio."

Balestrini gave a curt laugh and looked at Fran with a kind of condescending amusement. "It pays for her to be discrete in these days of democratic Italy. Her husband was quite an important Fascist leader under the regime. One of the *prominenti*. The partisans got him among the first. Yes, with such a history it pays to lie low and have students cover you with respectability and pay you rent."

Fran was annoyed. Was he trying to make her appear guilty by association? "Well, I didn't know, and what does it matter anyhow? She had an ad in the Rome Daily American and my business is with her, not her dead husband."

"Yes, and you have a comfortable place, plenty of quiet, with room for your books, and," as he picked up a mug inscribed *L'homme est un fleuve, la femme un lac*, "even your mottos."

"Not my motto," she said, "just a souvenir from when I was at Lake Geneva."

It was a good room, large and clean and filled by day with glorious Roman light and by night with thick Roman quiet. It easily accommodated the large garland-painted wardrobe that stood in the far corner near the long shuttered window, a bureau, a table-desk and bookcase, and even a settee and chairs grouped around a low table opposite her divan-bed.

Balestrini, as she knew he would, walked around examining things. He stopped at an illustration torn from a magazine that was tacked over the bookcase. "Lady Talbot, by the Flemish painter Petrus Christus," he read. He stepped back and scanned the portrait of a pale young woman in medieval garb whose head was covered by a black toque, which wrapped under her chin and hid her hair except for the minutest brown fringe showing at the edge of her very wide forehead. Her eyes slanted and looked coldly and appraisingly to the side; her mouth, small and closed, was set and resolute. Around her white throat was an exquisite five-strand necklace alternating gold chain with diamonds. An ermine-lined robe sloped off white shoulders. She was a study in calm and cunning, in unfathomable hauteur.

"A patron saint?" the professor inquired lightly.

34

He was teasing but, in fact, he had gotten it right. It was the picture that had accompanied Fran all through college. It was the depiction of an admonition she had once given herself: You are safe if you don't give yourself away—if no one knows who you really are. Keep the mystery. Keep yourself closed.

"No," she lied. "I just like it.

A pair of skis and poles leaned against the side of the bookcase. Balestrini picked up a large blue volume of Kierkegaarde and opened it. In Fran's hand was written: *Odi et amo/quare id faciam, fortasse requiris/Nescio. sed fieri sentio et excrucior.* "I hate and I love?" he asked, raising his brows. "Strong words." He picked up Lear's *Book of Nonsense* and looked inside and found the same quote.

"Ah yes," he said as came back to the center of the room where Fran stood watching him, "you have everything. Is this painting yours, too?" He was looking at a portrait that hung over the settee. It was the head and bust of a young man who was looking instensly off into the distance, his eyes crinkled with attention. His face was lean and his cheek bones pronounced. His hairline already gave signs of receding and made for a wide forehead. It was an attractive face and an alert one which forced the question, what is he thinking, what plan is he devising? The lifelike head was set off by a wierd background of colors, which shot off in rays like a kaleidoscopic aureole. The colors were jarring—harsh pink, lurid green, black, muddied yellow. But they were applied with a painstaking precision that gave their wildness a formality and disturbingly emphasized the head around which they converged. "This man in the painting," Balestrini went on, "is he the one?"

Fran turned away, flinging her coat on a chair.

"Yes, he's the one." She looked at the painting of Walter, which she had done from a photo of him sitting on a tree stump, one knee over the other. "I did it from a snapshot he gave me. He was on a forestry expedition. He's sort of scowling because the sun is in his eyes."

"I see. The scowl is good for him—it gives him an interest that young men don't usually have. Perhaps he should never smile. But I didn't know you were an artist."

35

"I'm not, really. I just copy." She said this impatiently. She wished he would go, and said as if to discourage him, "I can only offer you some Pernod." She did not ask him to remove his coat.

"You <u>are</u> strange," he laughed.

"Well, you are strange, too," she replied. "So different now from what you are in the classroom."

"Of course," he said jovially. "But the stuffy academic professor is the fake. This is what I really am—the buffoon, the nighttime prowler, the seducer of young girls!"

Balestrini watched Fran go to the bookcase for the Pernod and two bright earthenware cups. Why, he wondered, had she asked him in? So that he could see, firsthand, the portrait of her love? It was not passion but fantasy and romance that engaged her. What she liked about the whole business, he suspected, was its never being realized.

Fran handed him his drink in the earthenware cup. "I'm sorry," she said, "this is not the way to serve Pernod, but I have nothing else and it's too late to call the maid for some glasses."

"Decidedly not the way," Balestrini agreed, shaking his head at the Deruta earthenware which all visitors to Italy seemed to collect. "Drinking liqueur in terracotta painted with wreaths and roosters is not done. But nothing of what you are doing is done."

He raised his cup to the painting. "To the great unknown!" he toasted.

"What do you think of it?"

Balestrini turned to her without the smile or air of mockery he had worn most of the evening. "It is interesting you know. I don't think I have ever seen such a frigid painting. These colors are like El Greco when he gets ice into his pinks and takes all warmth from yellow."

"And yet that is what he looks like."

"That's not what I mean. As a portrait of him I suppose it's all right—it's as a portrait of you that it's disturbing."

"Why?"

"You're attempting to show the strength of your feelings. But what you show is actually only something you've artfully constructed. Your love is a game—if it weren't, why wouldn't his snap-shot and your memories of him be enough?"

"I liked doing the painting."

"I'm sure. What you love most in this affair is yourself."

"So many theories—so professorial!" she countered, emboldened by the strong liqueur.

"My wish for you is that someday you'll love a man you won't have to invent."

She couldn't bear him trying to analyze what she knew and felt. "What else is love but invention?"

"Maybe you're right," he sighed, getting up from the settee. He faced the painting and raised his cup. "Let's drink to your friend, and let's give him a name. Let's call him Cassius—he looks like Shakespeare's fellow, 'Yond Cassius has a lean and hungry look; he thinks too much—such men are dangerous.'"

Balestrini finished his drink, pleased both by the warmth of the Pernod and his ease in quoting English. "One more question about Yond Cassius, and then *basta*. What is written on his tunic?"

"It's a tee-shirt, it says School of Forestry."

"Cassius is American? What is he doing in Rome, is he with the Embassy or the United Nations Food and Agriculture Agency?"

Balestrini started to sit down again but shook his head at the settee and, raising his eyebrows in a look of query at Fran, inclined his head toward her divan-bed across the room. It was strewn with cushions and the floral print of the spread was repeated in a wall tapestry tacked along its length and across the head, making the corner a comfortable flowered bower.

Fran nodded and settled herself among the cushions. Balestrini followed, slumping down in a half recline with his head against the wall. Fran looked across the room at the painting and shook her head. "No, he's as Italian as you—he's from Ancona."

"Ah! beware of those from the Marche region -they have a bad reputation: *meglio un lupo alla porta che non un marchigiano in casa.*"

"A wolf at the door—what a thing to say! Italians have spiteful sayings for anybody from a different hometown. Anyway, he lives in Rome now."

Fran, sipping the warming anise drink, was glad to be talking about Walter. She had never spoken of him to anyone after the one painful try with her mother. Her mind flicked for an instant to the house in Philadelphia—how remote it seemed.

"A government official decided to send him to the states after the war for an update in forestry," she continued. "My father invited him home for Thanksgiving. I thought he was Swedish when I met him—he was tall, serious, and studying Forestry. How could I know there were Italian foresters?" Fran smiled at the reminiscence.

"So, that was the first let-down, that your Swede turned out to be Italian," Balestrini laughed.

"Not at all, he got me interested in learning Italian. He got me here. I owe him a lot. I didn't know until too late that he had a wife."

"Now you're here waiting. Like patient Griselda. A wait can be a hard thing when you're alone in a strange land." Gently, Balestrini slipped his arm around her shoulder. "What does your family say of the situation."

"Oh, my family! It's not the kind of thing we discuss. Officially I'm here writing travel accounts for the paper back home. It makes my parents happy to see my name in the paper."

"How strange you Americans are. It's as if you all come into the world to be loners, not to make connections with others."

But the strange thing for Fran was to hear herself over and over again categorized as one of 'you Americans' whom the professor knew from his readings. He didn't distinguish her as Italian American. He had no idea how precarious her identity as American was.

She felt his arm. She felt warmed by the Pernod, comfortable, and so she said, "And if my family knew about you, *professore?*"

"Don't worry, I won't let you get into trouble. I'll teach you everything, except to hate me."

"But if the classes are to stop?"

"Never mind about the classes. They aren't necessary to learn Italian. We'll go about Rome. I'll take you to Tivoli, to the Castelli Romani in the Alban hills—Frascati, Rocca di Papa, Marino. When it's warmer we'll go to Ostia Antica and Fregene and Nettuno and eat fresh fish in the sunlight. We'll go to all the *feste* in Rome and outside, too. We'll go wherever you wish!"

"*Bellissimo!* I could write my pieces about all those places. Then I could stay here forever!"

"Yes, you are clever," Balestrini said in amusement. "Not only pretty, but clever. Your age?"

"Twenty-two."

What he knew of American women he knew through literature and films. They were bold and confident, but always the ingénue. They didn't mature, they simply became older. Their appeal was short and Frances Molletone might be at the peak of hers.

"Your articles are a splendid idea," he said. "You can stay on as a journalist, not a student. It's more distinguished. Before spring we can go to Gran Sasso and I'll show you the Abruzzi of D'Annunzio and where Mussolini was rescued from his prison by German paratroopers. You were even clever enough to bring your skis with you so we can ski at Gran Sasso."

Fran looked at him astounded. "This is unbelievable—what about your wife?"

"Let me try to explain things. I couldn't have had Marisa -my wife- without marrying her. And I wanted her because she was suitable and of good family. That's all an Italian wife has to be, and my friends married exactly the same kind of woman. After a few years of marriage I cordially disliked Marisa while respecting and honoring her as the mother of our children. From then on I began the succession of pastimes I call my 'little loves' and to write erotic poetry. So you see, my wife and I go nowhere together except in the summer to her family place in the north. Each year at this time when *carnevale* starts I go off someplace to read and rest on my own while she indulges in her social life. She's glad to be rid of me and it's the period when I'm free from my university lectures. None of the people in the classes you attend will mind missing an evening or two during *carnevale*. But you will do the skiing, not I—I'll just be your chaperone."

He laughed as he tweeked her cheek, and Fran felt helplessly confused. Often in their letters, she and Walter had written of skiing and plans to do so together, but it had never been possible. Now she felt she wouldn't mind going off to Gran Sasso with the professor, just for a change. And then the absurdity hit her like the kick of the Pernod—would she actually start spending time with the professor just to be able to stay in Italy for Walter? The whole thing was crazy. She wriggled out of Balestrini's hold and stood up.

"It's really late, I think you'd better go. And a trip to Gran Sasso is impossible."

Balestrini grabbed a wrist and pulled her back down. He spoke harshly now: "Are you worried about your chastity? Why worry—no one wants it as far as I can tell."

He pushed her back among the cushions, pulled her face to his with both hands and kissed her vehemently. It was a hard, mocking kiss. He released her and got up as she lay there, feeling smothered and breathless. "Good night to you and Cassius here in your shrine," he said as he went through the door. She heard his footsteps in the hall, heard the great outer door open and close.

She glanced across the room to Walter's portrait and effortlessly succumbed to her memory.

They were at the dry kiln, a small building off the faculty parking lot behind the College of Forestry, at night. She was wearing a gray princess-cut coat with pretty buttons of blue stones set in a silvery metal. She wore fancy earrings to match the blue stones and she could see herself, sitting on a high stool, her legs crossed, one of her high-heeled black pumps resting on a rung. Walter, tall, wonderful, speaking in accented English about his problem of measuring shrinkage in the plank assigned to him, had brought her there, where a high stack of planks were piled outside, before they went on to a nearby bar.

"What a country," he was saying, "here everyone has his own plank to measure and his own personal shrinkage problem. In Italy we were twenty men to a plank." He laughed and opened a heavy, bolted door and went into a steamy place. Emerging, he went to an open notebook on a stand, then turned to her and said, "I have no pencil."

"Nor nineteen other men to borrow from—that's the price of being on your own the American way."

"Don't talk so much, you American girl."

"Here, use this," she said, handing him her lipstick.

He took it and pulled the top off with a swift, sucking sound. He turned the base slowly and watched the color come up. He held the tube near his nose. "Yes," he said looking at her lips, "it should be nice—like crushing wild strawberries on your mouth."

"You are a forester, not a poet, get on with your work. If it was so urgent that we had to stop here so late just to measure a bit of wood!"

"Urgent, yes. But not in the way you think."

"What kind of course is it," she said, simulating impatience, "that makes you come way out to this place? Does every guy get a girl with a car?—or is that just for European students as a kind of propaganda?"

"It is merely my good fortune," he said as he wrote in the notebook with the lipstick. "The same kind of fortune that makes your father so eager to ask foreign students to his house for Thanksgiving and then, besides the turkey, presents a nice daughter as well. Did I ask for any of it?"

"With all this good fortune over here you shouldn't go back to Italy."

"No," he said, giving her a long look. "You know, my father used to say, 'When I might have, I could not... now that I can, I may not'—I think it's from Goethe."

She said nothing more, but got up from the stool and went to the blackboard where she a made a sketch of him embracing a plank. When he finished his notation in the notebook, he replaced the top onto the lipstick tube and came over to her. "Why do you waste me on such a piece of wood?" he asked with a smile, looking at the drawing. "Now try out some Italian—write, I love you."

She drew a balloon above the plank and wrote in it *Ti voglio bene*. Walter was directly behind her, watching her closely. He said softly, "Yes, you would write it that way, you keen sharp American graduate; it's not as much as *Ti amo* -you don't give up everything at

41

once." He smiled in a slow way and put his hands on her shoulders. "You are nice... really nice," he said. Then they left the dry kiln.

In the car, when he kissed her, she had ducked her face onto his shoulder and after some silence he had said very softly, "You are very precious to me. Do you feel the same way?" She nodded without raising her head and they stayed there, close together, for a time.

Then they went to a place called Luigi's Italian Village in an old and decaying neighborhood down the hill from the University. Luigi's, a bar with a dance-floor, had once been a house like others on the street until its plain clapboard exterior was stuccoed over and an archway created at its entrance to give the place a Mediterranean look -a hopeless enterprise on that gray bleak street.

Dancing closely, at a certain moment they had stopped and looked into each other's eyes, taken, in the same instant, by knowledge that flowed through them. Embraced on the dance-floor, he had brushed his lips against her ear, her temple, her eyes. Without a word they understood everything. She was sure then of what love was.

But that same night as they sat with their drinks, perhaps recklessly driven by the dark, searching part of her nature, the part that couldn't believe in her good fortune, she had looked at him across the table and said in a voice husky with surprise, "You're married."

He pushed his drink aside and looked back at her steadily,. "Yes, I'm married," he said finally, "does it matter?"

And because everything had just burst and nothing not only mattered, but nothing was, she shook her head, "No." Stunned to silence, shocked, she fell back into the trance-like mask that hid her feelings. Like Lady Talbot, whose portrait she had in her room, who revealed nothing. Sang-froid. Fran knew how to dissemble, it was her way of getting past painful moments and now it helped her resurface as she sportingly played out the evening.

"Show me her picture."

"I haven't one."

"What is her name?"

"Lucia—but what does it matter?"

"I'm just curious. When were you married?"

He sighed, looked resigned, and lit a cigarette. "It was during the war. I'd known her all my life in Ancona and had always seen her—on the beach, strolling in the center, watching the basketball games I played in, everywhere. It was natural for me to marry her at that moment, I didn't even have to think about it. Four years ago everything was in a mess, you couldn't be sure of anything—whether you would live or die, what people would be left in your town from one day to the next, or if the town would be there. We were being bombed, the British and Americans were advancing and the Germans digging in. I managed to get to the British forces and become an interpreter for them. When we got near Ancona, they let me borrow a jeep and I took Lucia out of the city and we were married in some country place. Two days later I was back fighting, then in prison, and I didn't see her again until the war was over. We moved to Rome where I had work and then the Ministry sent me here. My marriage seems something I can't even remember at times."

He was married, and he wanted to make love to her, to spend what time was left before he returned to Italy with her.

At home that night, alone, she cried. Aching with desire and hurt and unsure of what to do, she cried for her loss. There seemed nothing left for her, only the satisfaction that Walter hadn't seen her cry; to him she had merely said no, his being married didn't matter. She told herself she would never let him know how much it did.

She did not sleep that night. Her thoughts swept through her like a dizzying, stinging dust storm, her hopes whirling about her like desert debris. Still, he loved her; she had felt it. For him love was reason enough for them to be together; but she wanted a future not a brief encounter and then being left alone with no ties to anything while he returned to his work, his wife, his country and the sweet memory of his American adventure. She would have the same memory, but bitter.

She could not do it. It was not enough for her to have a few nights of love and then nothing. He had started something in her -

some new way of looking at the world and of thinking of herself - that she did not want to be stopped.

In Rome, more than a year and several thousands of miles from the dry kiln and from Luigi's, Fran still felt the impact Walter's words had made on her when he said, Does it matter? Dull and heavy as thuds, like monstrous things sitting on her chest, they left her breathless. She could feel again the savage thumping in her breast that had been the crazy panic of her heart that night at Luigi's.

She couldn't help herself: she was remembering it all. It was Thanksgiving and her father was saying, "This is Walter Bongalli, he's from Italy."

"That's an unusual name," she responded.

"Why?" He regarded her with amused insolence. He was tall and lean-cheeked and his look was intent. "You know we have a few unusual names in Italy, too -just as a relief from all the Giuseppes and Antonios. Do you think my hair has to be black as ink and I have to be wearing a waiter's suit for me to be Italian?"

"No... no, of course not!" she flushed with embarrassment at being so gauche. "I don't know much about Italy. My grandparents came from there but I was never able to speak to them."

"Well, you should go to Italy—you would find that we are not all jolly fishermen who spend days in the sun singing O *sole mio*. In Italy you would see that the women are not all short and fat and dressed in black—they wear makeup and shoes and even have more style than Americans."

His sarcasm was veiled by a pose of polite affability. Fran watched him talk with her father and the other guests, always courteous, yet with a sharp edge to his words. At the dinner table when Frank Molletone had pointed to the huge turkey and said to Walter, "You don't see anything like this in the old country," Fran had felt indignant. But glancing across the table at Walter she was struck by his composure.

"No," Walter had answered his host, "we don't have such enormous birds as these in Italy, but we have a few other things, you know. It would have been nice during my prison stay to see how long I could have made such a turkey last. I used to do that with the bread they gave us each day. The other prisoners would eat it all at once, but I would portion mine out, bit by bit, over the whole day."

Fran thought of her mother's basement hoard of rationed foods accumulated during the war: sugar, coffee, tuna fish and olive oil were still stored in the basement. "Prison, how awful!" she exclaimed. "Why were you there?"

"No, it was not awful," Walter answered easily. "It was war when I was caught on the wrong side and the Fascists had no choice but to put me in prison, which from their point of view I deserved. It was a time in my life that I did a lot of thinking—probably the most that I'll ever do, and I've always been glad for that. I got used to being there and I even felt sorry to leave my cell and my bedbugs and my daily bread. That weak part of me was sorry even for something I had no reason to like. You can imagine how I am when I really like something." He looked at Fran when he said this and his smile was lazy, inviting, provocative.

"That was Mussolini's one mistake," her father said, gesturing with his fork, "getting into war on the wrong side. He should have stopped while he was ahead, then everything would have been all right."

Fran hated her father's remarks. She remembered when a stricken, invaded Italy abandoned its German partner and surrendered to the Allies, and how her father had jeered at the Italians as cowards and good-for-nothings. Until she heard Walter describing the war she had never heard of Italian partisan fighters or of the self-exiled anti-fascists who were distinguished Italian writers and scientists, some of them living in the states.

"Well, there are some of us in Italy who think he made some other mistakes, too," Walter answered dryly.

Walter and her father then got immersed in talk of the war and of how the Allied troops had re-taken the country. Walter was intelligent, sophisticated, caustic and her father was impressed despite himself. The Italian student refuted by his mere presence the legend of a despicable Italy that Frank Molletone, the son of poor and unschooled immigrants, carried within and passed on. He asked Walter what his father did and nodded respectfully at the word lawyer. And Walter spoke not only of his father, but of his mother and brother and sister as well. But never of a wife.

He had a part-time job in a downtown hotel and had to leave on Thanksgiving day before the others. When Fran offered to drive him in her Chevy, her mother drew her aside and said, "Now don't go getting interested in any Italian! I know what I'm saying, the way he's talking, he's probably a communist."

In the car, Fran asked in amusement, "Are you, as my mother thinks, a communist?"

He laughed. "Your mother is a nice-looking lady, but not too clever. I am not a communist—I am not any kind of a revolutionary. Just briefly during the war I knew what I had to do. But mostly I am just a forester and my motto is 'Simple but dignified", just as the motto of such a wooden person should be. You mother would be disappointed that I am so ordinary, but that's how it is. Sometimes, but only sometimes, I am myself. Most of the time I am watching what is going on in the world, then waiting for the best offer."

"What kind of offer?"

"Any kind—even one from you."

His manner excited her. He gibed at all of them, then watched the effect with a quizzical look that continued the baiting. And yet he was so steady, so composed around some true center of his being that she felt, by contrast, like the cartoon of an empty-headed American co-ed. He was unlike anyone else she knew.

"What is this job I'm driving you to?" she asked.

"I am a busboy, I bus," he said.

"Oh."

"Yes, not a very chic job in your eyes but it has been for me a most interesting period in my life. The other night I did something I was tempted to do since I started work in the hotel -I refused a tip. I was tired of seeing all the waiters and other busboys jumping like frogs to get those bits and scraps of change. I gave the tip back to the man whose glass I had filled and said, 'I am sorry, Sir, I do not want it.' He looked at me and said, 'What's wrong with you?' Poor guy—

46

he meant what's right with you and he didn't know it. That's my life as a busboy. I shall be sorry to leave it when Christmas vacation starts. Do you know something about me yet? I am foolish and senti-mental and the last days are always sad for me no matter what ends and what may start."

"Then why will you leave your job."

"My time in America is over and I shall miss America, too. I go back to Italy at the end of this semester."

"So soon?"

He looked intently at her as if trying to penetrate her thoughts. "Unfortunately, I have already been here a year before meeting you. But there is still some time for us."

They met when they could between his studies and part-time job and her work in a downtown advertising office. Once he came to meet her on her lunch hour, and said "I got a phone call last night and I thought it was you."

Proudly, she said, "I would never call you."

"Why?"

"Why?—because the man should do the calling. It's not up to me to lead the way."

"Oh, I see," he said and she could hear the amusement in his voice, the kind one has for a child who has said something funny without knowing it. "So, you are afraid to look like a leader for a phone call. You are lying, my girl. You told me the other night that you went to the library with the idea of paying me a visit afterwards. In that case you would have run the risk of looking like half a dozen leaders. I like liars -especially when they look like you, with your green eyes- but when they are caught I like to hear, 'Yes sir, I lied. So? I felt like lying and I did.' You see, my girl, the thing to be, always, is an open, sincere liar."

"Are you that kind?"

"No. Just a blooming liar. But now I will tell you the truth. I haven't kissed you yet and maybe you know why. But if you don't, don't worry. There is nothing wrong with you, it is only that I don't like the predictable in that sort of thing. It doesn't mean that I wouldn't like to—I get a kind of pleasure just thinking about it. But to do a nice job both persons have to want it so I am just waiting and watching for the right moment. You know, I am still young, I have time."

"No," she said, more seriously than she intended, "you seem to me older than anyone I've ever talked to before."

"Then I am Methuselah, and this is the beginning of my nine hundred and sixty-nine years—with you."

Behind the banter and his teasing urbaneness, there was both sincerity and pretense. It was this shading in him, this fact of not being transparent and common, that enticed her. Fran loved everything about him—the sensuality of his lean, taut face; the feel of his hands on hers; the things he said, the responses he elicited from some long-closed storeroom of repression in her. She liked the part of him that was thoughtful and candid, but even what was egotistical, cynical, ambiguous.

It was with Walter that she most fully realized how cramped she was in her little world with its limited sights and its fear of not being like everyone else. Now she was sure of the emptiness of her home, of a family with whom she had no spiritual kinship. He sharpened the edge of her discontent and put into relief the littleness of the people she had always known. Walter gave her her first glimpse of what Italian really was.

"Teach me Italian!" she had begged one night with such a strong, imploring tone that he laughed at her. "I want to go to Italy," she said.

He dug in his pocket for change and held out a handful of coins to her. "Here is something for your trip, I never know what to do with these pennies. Just in case your father doesn't like the idea."

"It doesn't matter if he does or not, I'll save the salary from my job."

All the restlessness of her life was focused and concretized by Walter. Now she understood that always present sense of sadness that was so much a part of her, the sense of not belonging and of not knowing who she was, the shame of being someone not right. She saw in Walter the way out of the endless circle. She wanted to leave and go where she could come into being again.

She had even thought of leaving with Walter when he did.

But the end had come. As long as she lived, she thought, she would hear him say, Yes, I am married, does it matter?

Up to that moment everything had a worth; after, everything became an enormous taunt. The newly engaged couple in her office made her physically sick; the Christmas decorations all over downtown repelled her. Tears would come to her eyes at work, suddenly and without provocation, and she would have to turn her face to avoid being seen.

As the sadness became too great, some survival reflex began converting it to anger. Why, on Thanksgiving day, hadn't he mentioned his wife? Why had he waited until it was too late and then only said, Does it matter? As Fran replayed the scenes over and over, she began to hate what he had done to her. This brought relief and new purpose: she would hurt him as she had been hurt.

Walter had arranged his Christmas vacation to spend some extra time with her before going to New York to leave for Italy. Now she decided he would spend those days alone, thinking of her. She would go out with him for the last time; she would talk as if nothing had happened, they would dance, they would make plans.

Again they went to Luigi's. She could tell that he had not the slightest notion of the turmoil inside her; rather, he sensed an excitement and abandon in her that made her all the more desirable. Dancing, she put both arms around his neck and they whispered to each other. "How nice you look tonight," he said, "you have a soft, sleepy look... a look like a cat. A cat with green eyes."

They sat close to each other, their hands entwined. He had fingered the ring on the middle finger of her left hand, three oval turquoise stones set in a thick silver band. "Who gave you this?" he asked.

"I had it made in Mexico," she said, "I gave it to myself."

He laughed. "Yes, I think that would mean a lot to you."

She had then taken his right hand in hers and studied it closely, as if to memorize it. "You talk like a Frenchman," she told him, "you look Swedish, and you have Spanish hands."

"And you have shadows and light under that lace that tempt me and I'm afraid I can't do anything about it in this moment."

"And what is there to do?"

"You know what there is to do, and it isn't so easy as to talk. When I am speaking to you, like this, you have nothing to do but listen, to stay close near my shoulder and let me smell your perfume and look into your eyes that are like green velvet. But in the other case your should participate, and so far you haven't except on two occasions—when I kissed you at the dry kiln and when we danced for the first time."

"There's no time for anything more than a look, or a drink, or a last dance. Italy is waiting for you."

"And you?"

"No, not I. I am not waiting for you or anyone!" She had laughed at him and teased him, fencing with him, letting him approach and then turning him away.

"I love you like this," he said, "because I can't be sure. I don't know what the hell is going on but there's hell in your eyes and I like it. You are soft like a cat, but I can feel your claws, too. When I think you are at rest, then you spring. And when you look at me with your head a little down like that, it's better than a caress... better, almost, than an invitation."

She hadn't smoked that night at Luigi's; she had given it up she told him to test her will power.

"And does your will power mean more to you than such a small pleasure?"

"Yes. What means more to you?"

"You." She knew it was true. If part of her was coolly fencing, a deeper part still loved him as she always would. To steel herself, she kept in mind that his encounter with her was only one of his souvenirs of America.

They were to go to his place. At her car she turned to him and said, "I'm going home now. I won't see you again."

He stood there stunned. "But you have been so warm tonight... you made me believe...."

"Make-believe. Never believe a liar, as you once said, even a sincere one."

"You knew this when you came out with me tonight? You knew this was our end?" It had started to snow. He stood there quietly looking at her, the light snow dusting his hair, his shoulders. "I have to go back a long time in my life before I remember another night when I felt for anyone what I felt for you tonight. You know it. We had so little time left. Less than a week. But you had to convince yourself you're strong—now I understand your precious will power. You have stolen this time from both our lives. I just hope you won't regret it later...."

She had driven away, leaving him standing in a whirl of snow-flakes that fluttered out of the dark night, swirled for a moment under the streetlight and settled onto the frozen ground.

The next day she got his special delivery letter: "I didn't wash my hands last night before going to bed. I didn't because I had your perfume in my hands. I could smell you and it meant something to me last night. Your perfume is good, it doesn't hurt, it just pleases. I love it. I love you. I thought how I could keep your scent with me, but life with its regulations will defeat me just as it did last night. I will take a shower and your perfume will be gone. It will slip out of my hands just as you did a few minutes ago. The perfume cannot come back, but you can if you want. If you want—that is the rub."

In the days that followed she got other letters, long ones of his loneliness and longing. His pain assuaged hers. The day he sailed for Italy he sent her a post-card on which he wrote, There's always the next time. And on it his office address in Rome.

That winter she studied Italian with Mr. di Tomasi, and she painted Walter's portrait from the snapshot she had of him.

From Rome he wrote her, once sending a cartoon from Punch that showed a Biblical personage being interviewed by a tweedy re-porter who said, I'm from the Institute of Public Opinion, Mr. Methuselah. Do you consider controls will ever be lifted in our life-time?

Beneath that Walter had written: "Will you come. I have been waiting for your so long that I am now restless. Don't worry in Rome if you don't see me at first glance—I'll see you at the second."

Fran awoke as Amelia the maid entered the room with her breakfast tray.

"Is it a good day, Amelia?" she asked the thin dark woman who put down the tray on a low table next to the bed.

"*Ai, me,*" Amelia, muttered wearily in reply, rolling her eyes upward, her long face skeptical as she slithered over the terrazzo pavement in her worn felt slippers and threw open the shutters, letting in the bright sun of a clear, chill day.

"A good day?—they're all the same." Amelia was agile and wiry and probably no more than in her thirties though she looked immeasurably older, her eyes sunken in her thin face and darkened by shadows. Her dark, straight hair was lank and straggly and her expression was one which asked no quarter and gave none. She came from across river, the Trastevere section of Rome whose inhabitants were said to be the last true remnants of the ancient city's populace. Rome, like New York, was where everyone lived and worked but where few were native born.

"Well, tomorrow is Sunday," Fran told her, "and that's different for you."

"*O, ben,*" Amelia retorted sourily. "Big difference—a few hours liberty to walk in the park with *Il Baffone,* the scoundrel! Men! They're all bad except the pope, the king, and *il duce*—and look what happened to him."

Amelia reserved her most caustic disapproval for men even as she passed the day wailing sentimental love songs and plaintive dirges of passion throughout the apartment she alone had to keep up. Whenever the duchess wasn't about, she telephoned the man she called *il Baffone*—the Big Moustache—to chide and accuse him and ask him how many new love affairs he was busy with since they last met. After the rapid outburst of her indignation, there must have always been something soothing on the other end of the line for

Amelia, placated, would go back to the kitchen to sing again of love. Fran admired the resilience that lay beneath Amelia's skepticism.

Fran sat up in bed and looked with little enthusiasm at the invariable breakfast tray. It held a hard roll, a curl of butter and a dab of marmalade, and two little pitchers one containing boiled milk and one strong coffee which she would pour together into a cup for her *caffè-latte*. That's me, she thought. A something which is no longer plain milk, but never gets coffee-ish enough. Not pure American, never Italian enough. A *cappuccino*. Even the monkish name fits me.

Sipping her *caffè-latte* Fran admired the housemaid's capacity for a tough appraisal of her love affair. In her own case, she felt, the advantage was all on Walter's side now that she was in Rome. She wished, unreasonably, that things could be as simple as they were with Amelia and *Il Baffone*, that she could scoff as Amelia did but still, deepdown, be sure.

"Men—puh!" Amelia grumbled. "Even the Americans I read about in *Confessione*. They are not so treacherous as Italians but they are generally impotent or foolish. Just the same I would go to America. But since there's no chance of my finding a Columbus to take me there, I'll stick with *Il Baffone*. And you, *signorina*," she added as she picked up the two sticky cups near the bottle of Pernod, "did you go out walking last night?"

Damn, Fran chided herself, annoyed at having left those remains of the past evening in sight. It was no good denying that someone (and of course Amelia would assume a man) had been in her room last night, so she might as well hint at Walter. Amelia knew him from the painting and an occasional telephone call. As long as she thought it was Walter who had been there, Fran was sure she wouldn't mention it to the duchess. In the sisterhood of women with troublesome male partners, Amelia had come to regard Walter as Fran's equivalent of *il Baffone*.

"*Il dottore* came in for a drink and left even before the front gate was locked."

Amelia nodded and mournfully repeated, "Ah, men!" as she left the room.

Fran stayed in her room all morning. *Dear Mr. di Tomasi,* she wrote, *Italy just after the war is a fine place to be. Americans haven't discovered it yet, and the Europeans who have money to travel, like the Swiss and Swedes are waiting for the clutter and inconveniences left by armies and bombers to be cleared away before they come. The Germans are not yet in any shape to be tramping through the boot, making camp sites from the Dolomites to the Straits of Messina. And the Italians themselves are full of cheefulness and inventiveness -as if hard times and a destroyed land make them resourceful rather than bitter. As if another great age in their long history will come out of all this. It's the sense of freedom after the regime of oppression that makes the austerity they are going through well worth it. They adapt to the difficult times with ingenuity and good spirits and a great deal of humanity. How proud I am to be here at this very moment!*

It was true, Fran thought, as she concluded her letter to Mr. di Tomasi, and, her confidence high, began thinking of her newspaper piece. She loved being in Rome; she no longer felt estrangement as her deepest reality.

She typed out random thoughts on her portable from college: *Ingrid Bergman is here with the film director Roberto Rossellini, and a huge barefoot and bearded Messiah came from Mozambique to try to see the Pope. There is the ancient city, the proud capital of emperors whose memories hang on in the forums, in the arches inscribed Caesar Dux, and even in attitudes such as that of the railroad porter I hired for my baggage who deigned only to beckon to a sub-porter to do the hauling for ten percent of the tip while the first porter walked alongside me and chatted.*

Yes, Rome, the eternal paradox, the successful amalgam of old and new, staid and bizarre. A city swarming with government clerks from the South, businessmen from the north, titled absentee landlords, farmers moving in from the provinces, the foreign diplomatic services, clergy from all nations, international opportunists, and movie aspirants also from everywhere. The catacombs of Sant'Agnese just down the street from where I live, and Barbasol shave cream sold from open suitcases by hawkers on the Spanish Steps beneath the window of the room where John Keats died; the red-robed seminarians who swish through narrow streets on their way to orations and the red kerchiefed communists under the leadership of Togliatti the wiley; custom limousines pass sheep grazing near the Baths of Caracalla and leaving their turds on stones from two millenia ago; on the Appian Way there are the footprints of denying St. Peter in the pavement and next door the Quo Vadis auto-repair garage.

And all of Baroque Rome—the heroic fountains of Bernini, Salvi, and Fontana; the noble palazzi, the great basilicas. Rome de luxe: the sycamores of Via Veneto, the shop windows full of expensive chic, the Hotel Excelsior where soon-to-be-married Tyrone Power is staying, the midday parade of snobs to Doney's cafe where I once overheard a fashionable woman say to a well-dressed man, What I lack is a sense of infinity.

Sunday in Rome: the bells and chants and incense of a thousand churches. And the afternoon promenades of all the Amelias and Baffones, as stately and slow as a Bach passacaglia as they meander through the center and linger, window by window, at all the fine shops. The parks are full on Sunday—children, balloon men, chestnut vendors, lovers. The stadiums are full, cafes are full. All Rome spills out into the streets, the city throbs with a vital force. And I remember how bare Sunday was in Philadelphia with a sense of desolation in the abandoned downtown streets as if only week-day people going to work gave the city any meaning.

Fran stopped to consider: the shame towards Italy she had felt in Philadelphia had been learned at home and in the evil-smelling groceries on the South Side where funny people spoke the rough, ugly sounds of dialect that she had thought was Italian before she learned the language; or in films which showed gangsters who always had Italian names and spoke broken English.

In a perverse way, it had been Fascism, with its evocation of Imperial Rome and attempt to ape northern efficiency and get trains running on time, that had given Italian Americans a brief, ill-gotten sense of pride and some reprieve from the sense of inferiority conferred on them by the dominant Anglo-Saxon culture. 'What curious attitudes..., Alice exclaimed in *Beyond the Looking Glass*. Not at all, said the king..., those are Anglo-Saxon attitudes....'

By one-thirty when Amelia rapped on her door to announce dinner, Fran had finished a first draft of an article to send to the editor of the Philadelphia evening paper. Her work had absorbed her completely, giving her focus and sense of purpose. She began to love what she was doing. She felt she was achieving something, not merely passing time.

She was the last to be seated at table in the study where they took their meals. The two Englishwomen, Miss Pickers and Miss Gill, Tsui the Chinese student, and Maria Grazia and Gabriella the daughters of the house, were all in place. Usually, after polite salutations, they all sat in silence through the long meals while Amelia trudged back and forth, course after course, from kitchen to table. The teen-age girls were solemn and pale and too timid, or too indolent, to converse; Tsui made efforts, always grinning, but was often incomprehensible in English or Italian; and the English misses spoke only in undertones, only to each other, and only about the food: 'Isn't this lovely'... 'Grand, isn't it....'

But on this day Miss Gill was saying to Tsui, "Yes, life is hard in England just now, a little strict and pinched. It's better here because the Italian will never be one hundred percent serious about anything. The Italian—even the lowest field-hand—is an artist in temperament and this keeps him from total allegiance to anything. Of course the Italian will work like a madman when he works from the heart, but a little anarchy seems a good thing seen from here. The artistry of Florence, the history of Rome, the sun of Italy, well, after all, what more is there to want?"

"Quite," said Miss Pickers.

Fran thought how nicely the English had always achieved a compensatory balance with Italy. They brought an admiration to Italy that did not at all compromise their Anglo-Saxon attitudes but carried them successfully, chin up, through the opera buffa world of Italianness that Americans stopped to hoot at, and Italian Americans felt like a personal blemish.

"Austerity is good for us, I'm sure," Miss Pickers went on in her clipped U-tones. "Mr. Cripps is trying hard. But it's so much more agreeable being here."

"Indeed!" agreed Miss Gill. "How lovely the risoles are today. *Brava*, Amelia!"

"Are you thinking of going to England," Fran asked Tsui. "No, no. Oh, no," he said in a rush, showing his teeth, flustered by such a direct question.

Amelia who was clearing the table shook her head and muttered, "He doesn't have to go to England, what he needs is to leave his books and get a girlfriend." Tsui cut Amelia with a look of severe reproval, bowed shortly to Fran and left the room.

Fran shook her head at Amelia: "Poor Tsui, you frighten him with such an idea."

"Ai!" Amelia exclaimed, screwing her face in distaste. "*Che brutto* Signor Tsui with his flat nose! You can tell a man by his nose. Well let him amuse himself the best he can with his books, the rest of the world will make love until Judgment Day."

She's probably right, Fran thought. We're all caught in it some way or another, even by not being caught. What else is there?

And then she thought of her morning's work—yes, that had been good, too.

The chill of the *tramontana* which had swept through the plains of Latium and caught Rome in a penetrating cold, and which Fran had felt so sharply at St. Peter's the night before, was gone and the day was limpid with blue skies and puffs of clouds when she went out.

At the outer gate, the porter glanced from his window and waved. "*Buona sera*, Silvio, she called. He sighed "Ah, America!", part in banter, part in earnest, as she passed. She turned up the street towards Via Nomentana, a broad avenue lined with trees and some villas that ran from Porta Pia out to the country itself near Monte Sacro. Fran thought of how they all looked to America—Amelia, Silvio, her father's cousin Tino Molletone, strangers she met in trains, and even Walter who had what he called his crash with the states and was so restless and unsatisfied with his Ministry job in Rome. (Marry me! I'll give you America, came the refrain in her head.)

She was on her way to meet Walter. Passing a walled garden, Fran saw through a half-opened door a young nun in a white habit with a white starched bonnet throwing a ball against the wall.

Further up Via Nomentana, at Villa Torlonia where Mussolini had his residence and where the British War Graves Commission was now settled, the walls were covered with foot-high letters dripping paint: *Cristo scelse i suoi apostoli fra i lavoratori* it read, Christ chose his apostles among the workers. It was curiously mild as political graffiti went. For the walls of Rome were at that time covered with scrawlings that called for capitalists to be strangled with their own guts; threatened a blood-letting death to Mario Scelba, the Minister of the Interior whose police force was labeled assassins of the people. Garbed as a priest, Premier de Gasperi was shown hanging from gallows. Death was threatened to homosexuals who were accused of selling out to reactionary forces; Stalin was shown doubling for Garibaldi; the left-wing Nenni socialists squabbled with the socialists on the right, and the neo-Fascist M.S.I.party known as *missini*, hurled hate at them all.

Walter, the year before in the states, had been concerned with the political situation in Italy. It was touch and go whether the Communists would be the majority party or not. Pleas circulated in the United States for Americans of Italian origin to write to their relatives in Italy, urging them to vote for the Christian Democrats. Post-war Europe and America had been plunged into the cold war and Italy had the largest communist party in Western Europe.

Tension had been great preceding the first general election in the young Italian republic and Walter had written her from Ancona where he had gone to vote: "I voted. About an hour ago the elections were over. Now we are waiting for the results and we are anxious. These elections mean a lot to us—to me Italian, and to you American. I told people here what I could about America and if they don't like it, or if they don't believe it, it is no one's fault. It means that too many people were hungry and easily tricked. We have had to choose between USA and USSR and you know what my choice was."

Walter's letter had not been over-dramatic. From the states Fran had been caught up in the election furor and with Mr. di Tomasi's help had written to her grandfather's brother, Giuseppe Molletone, a retired civil servant living in Rome urging a vote against the communists. It was the old man's son Tino who answered her in a series of formalized salutations, good wishes for her health, and the hope to meet her someday.

She had sent clothes and CARE packages and began a correspondence with those relatives. She asked Tino about the political situation but he merely wrote back skeptically that all was wasted breath and energy. He had been a convinced fascist. In the end, the Italians voted for democracy.

Fran decided that her next piece for the hometown paper would be on the variety of political parties and views in Italy—it was a charged moment and the air was thick with opinion and discussion. It was also alive with a particular *brio* and surge of creativity as the spirit that had been dormant under the regime came alive in a renascence of writers, actors, directors, artists, fashion designers, craftsmen and architects that made Rome a center of ferment.

Via Nomentana ended in Porta Pia, a maelstrom of frenetic traffic. Motor scooters whined around the monument to the Bersagliere who had breeched the wall on September 20, 1870 in the final battle for Italian unification; trams and filobusses charged at pedestrians and the old clanking streetcars went by filled to the capacity of their buckling sides. Everything passed through the arch and into Via Venti Settembre.

It was *Carnevale*. Fran slowed her pace as she looked in store windows fascinatingly full of esoteric undergarments, lingerie and costumes, elegant suits. Fran herself dressed bizarrely—that day she wore green stockings, a belt studded with St. Christopher medals over a sweater embossed with a double-headed eagle, and the long skirts of the New Look, which Rome hadn't yet taken up. And with it all a beret from Paris and an enormous red shoulder bag that swung at her side. She was an eccentric among the Roman women in their trim *tailleurs*. She was someone different, not the person she had been.

Further ahead on Via Venti Settembre, towards Largo Susanna, were two large government buildings: on Fran's left the Ministry of Finances where Tino Molletone was employed, and on the right, diagonally across the street and equally gray and square, the Ministry of Agriculture and Forests where Walter had his office.

Fran thought of how different the two men were, Tino and Walter, and how alike were the offices where they worked, drab and filled with the same dusty bureaucratic odor of dull routine. Would it be only a question of time before Walter became as gray and pressed down as Tino and the other functionaries?

Fran left Via Venti Settembre and made her way to Via Veneto, the glamour street of Rome, passing Doney's cafe where devotees came at fashionable hours to have a drink, make contacts and let themselves be seen. She was heading for the great park at the end of Via Veneto known still by the name of the family who once held it as an estate, Villa Borghese. She was moved as always by the lovely filtered light, which slanted through the bending umbrella pines, deflecting the sun's rays in a diffusion of haziness. The pines of Rome. And around the park, the walls of Rome, old crumbled walls and arches of imperial Rome with plants sprouting from their rosy millennium bricks while the Fiat cars and Vespa motorbikes of modern Italy careened through them spilling themselves with noisy abandon and joy down Via Veneto.

The park in late afternoon was filled with children, with a balloon man, and still with some chestnut vendors. And there, too, under the statue of Goethe, dissolving her doubts of the previous evening like the smoke from his cigarette, was Walter. Every time she set out to meet him she feared he wouldn't be there, that the day would come, finally, when he'd no longer wait for her in Villa Borghese or in a cafe, or anywhere. But now as he glimpsed her and stood up watching her come toward him, Fran knew that time was still far off.

"*Ciao,*" he said, walking towards her with a wry smile. There was always a moment of reserve between them, a hesitation, a pause almost as if they, the players, were sizing each other up before the play began.

"Ah," she smiled, "you're wearing your American overcoat." He took her arm and they sat down on the pedastal at the foot of Goethe. He pulled a bag of chestnuts out of his pocket and offered them to her.

"Yes." He laughed. Fran loved the deepness of his laugh with its ring of self-mockery. He was wearing a gray-blue tweed coat that he had bought in Philadelphia and disliked ever since for it was too short and badly cut and not, as he said, dignified. "I am just waiting it to fall apart so that I can get a good Italian coat. But I am afraid it will not, this year or next." She loved the cadence of his English, the slowness and preciseness of how he chose his words.

"My father would be surprised at the idea of your preferring an Italian coat to an American one."

"Oh, yes, your father. And how is that prosperous man?"

"Prospering, I suppose. And carrying on as well as can be expected for someone who has a daughter in Europe and has to keep thinking of reasons for her being there because his friends can't understand it."

"He will have to accept."

"It's not so easy. He sends me newspaper clippings about people stranded abroad after losing their passports, or about flu epidemics, or propositioning openly carried on in the streets of Rome."

Walter chuckled. "Oh by all means—of course the open propositioning! It's much a part of Rome as the seven hills and I can swear I never saw one or the other."

"Most of all," she continued, "he's worried because the United States is sending so much money abroad through the European Recovery Plan and it's going to countries, he says, that are so rotten and corrupt they're past hope."

Walter shelled a chestnut with deliberation. Looking up at Fran, he said with a pseudo-earnestness, "Maybe he is right. Can you imagine a place with a big, rich life that is not corrupting and rotting? I know that place and it's not America, it's Utopia. If I had the money I would send your father and a few others there. In the meantime, maybe he would be kind enough to write some big-shots of the ERP and advise them to send us shipments of screws and bolts instead of dollars since we are falling apart. Then the American technicians could come over with their screw drivers to put us together because we not only fall apart, we stay apart—just sitting in the sun and watching girls go by."

"You're practically an American technician yourself."

"No. That's the trouble. They taught me to be one and I learned very well, but I am still Italian."

Walter thought how much more difficult it had been to come back and resume his life in Italy once he had had his crash with America. And then Fran had come, and what he liked best was her being America for him again.

"I, for one, am glad," she said softly. "And you shouldn't say my father is right, even for a joke. What does he know of things over here? Only what a reactionary columnist like Westbrook Pegler tells him."

"You know," Walter mused as if in a reverie, "we have a nice sense of fatality over here—*che sarà, sarà*—and we don't always feel obliged to be aggressive and try to rape destiny as you Americans do. There were some in Italy in the past twenty-five years who did try to be strong and aggressive and force things their way. Now we are just fed up with that kind of trying too hard."

He watched her shelling chestnuts, her air so placid, and wondered if she could understand.

"Sometimes it's so nice just to let things go.... You Americans can't understand that, you are too in a rush to keep things up despite gravity."

Fran wrinkled her forehead and looked at him, perplexed. "Why do you say, 'You Americans'? I have never felt like a real American. When I was in grade school, one of my friends asked me if I was Irish. I guess because we didn't live on the South Side where the Italians live. I wanted to say yes. Already then I knew it was better to be something other than Italian. I wanted to say yes, I'm Irish, but I couldn't. Later I found out that the Peters family, who lived next door to my grandmother Briciola, were actually named Pietrosasso. From then on they looked different to me, and how I thought about them was different, too. They weren't what they used to be."

"Poor thing! You don't know you're American!—it's only stamped all over you," he jeered derisively.

What he didn't see, she thought, was inside; but let it go. "Anyway," she went on, "I was in a rush to get here all my life without even knowing it. Now that I'm here, no more rushing around."

"What would your father say if you slowed down? Do you know what we should do to show we are a serious people?—we should pretend to rush and work nine to five as the Americans do because they can't understand people who do things differently. They're suspicious of us taking three hours off at noon even though we end up with more work time than they do. Still, it's un-American and therefore no good."

Fran listened to him silently; it's as if he were describing her life. She and her family were made to feel different from what the image of American was, as if only one image would do even in a country made up of people from all over. But in Walter's ingenuous version, they were suddenly part of the overall image.

He was still going on, enjoying himself. "We should rush to amuse ourselves, rush to get drunk, to relax, and even to make love. No sir, I can't agree! I want to stop from time to time just to look around and take notice of how the sun is shining or what the clouds look like in that particular moment—most of all, to find out what is my connection with the rest of the world in that moment. But it is foolish to talk this way—who gives a damn if your father and the others slow down or not?"

"Let's skip my father, it's too nice a day."

They fell silent, eating chestnuts.

She leaned back against the base of the statue, stretching her green-stockinged legs in front of her. Across the way from them two women strolled along the walk with that particular Italian grace she never failed to notice—half saunter, half lounge.

"How elegant the women of Rome are!" she said aloud. "They walk so well, they look so well. I used to think Italian women would all be wearing black baggy dresses and shawls. Instead they're more stylish than the women I saw in France or Switzerland—and much more than the Americans! I wonder how they keep so slim with all the pasta they eat everyday."

"Because they not only walk well, they make love well, too. Why don't you try it?"

Walter was looking at her teasingly, liking to watch her react. She looked placid, but he knew how easily she could be aroused—become unguarded, impulsive. He liked to test the tension between them as he used to measure it in planks in the dry kiln. He liked their different ways of skirmishing. He was in no hurry; he knew that when she finally gave in it would not only be the necessary completion they were both looking for, but the beginning of the end. At that point all women became the same; it was only before that there was some difference.

Reality meant less to him than what could be created, ideally, out of a situation; what pattern of ideas and symbols could be made to emerge from a person or circumstance that was, in itself, banal, was what interested him. He liked to detach a moment from its context and hold it, suspended, as long as possible. He enhanced experience by circling it slowly and not squandering it in too rapid an enjoyment.

As he supposed, Fran was offended and answered hotly, "Maybe I will try it -in Italy love is just as easy to find as pasta!"

He laughed and said dryly, "Yes, but unlike eating pasta love-making is usually more enjoyable in couples. Do you have a partner in mind?"

Goaded, Fran said impulsively, "Maybe. There's someone who's asked me to go skiing at Gran Sasso next week-end."

She could sting, Walter thought. And it was this, after all, that attracted him: the yes-no, the stop-go wrapped in a reticence that was, for him, deeply sensual.

"Well," he asked casually, "are you going?"

Furious at his nonchalance and sarcasm, Fran felt that if he had been angry, demanding, possessive, jealous—anything but what he was—she would have taken it better.

"Would you care?"

"What is there to care? Do I have any right to tell you what to do? That's something you have to know for yourself. You know there was a fellow at the Ministry who was in the office the last time you came and he said to me after you left, 'You are a son of a gun, Bongalli. Where did you find that nice girl? She is very nice and she looks like she likes you very much.' I could have told him what I was thinking—what I think every time I'm with you. I could have said, 'Don't worry about that girl—she knows very well how to make a person believe that she likes him very much. But that is not the whole truth—the whole truth is that she is a wonderful actress."

Fran was confused. He always seemed to reverse things. And yet he was also saying almost what the professor had said to her—theater, Balestrini said, she was making great theater out of simple attraction. She felt depressed and tired. Was all of this just an elaborate excuse to run away from home?

"I crossed the Alps for you. People at home said I should stay in Switzerland where it's safer."

"I don't think there's much Swissness in you."

"I like chocolate and skiing."

"And cuckoo clocks? Or predictable cuckoo-lives?"

"Not much."

"So you crossed the Alps for yourself, I'd say."

"And now, *che giuoco giuochiamo?*"

"I don't have a game, I have you," he said.

"Supposing, though, I had someone else, just as you have Lucia and maybe others. Supposing I wanted you but another, or others, in between."

"Yes," he laughed, "you could do it, too. You could make yourself be so sophisticated in a completely artificial way. But what is no good is that you have to force yourself to act in a certain way—none of it is simple and natural, that is the rub."

Yes, he could be natural about his wants in a way that she couldn't. Hadn't he already mentioned other women in the states before he met her? Hadn't he even joked with her about the list of women in Italy he would still like to make love to? None of it seemed immoral or dishonest to him. Only natural. It had made all her years of Latin very relevant. He was one with the culture that had produced Ovid and his *Ars Amatoria* where vigor and fantasy in love was more prized than constancy. He was part of the mentality of the novelist Brancati's *Il Bell'Antonio* which was then appearing in all the book-shop windows and, along with his previous *Don*

Giovanni in Sicilia, was the text par excellence (after Leporello's *'madamina, il catalogo è questo....'*) of the Italian male's Don Juanism. Was any Italian male exempt?

"Yes," she said pensively, wondering what would be left once the game was over. "Well, my friend forester, all is fair in love and war."

"And what do we have—the love or the war? Are you so interested in winning? I have already told you that with every couple -and it happens always- there is one who loves the other more than vice-versa. The one loving less is the winner. In our case you are already the winner, so why do you keep on fighting? What can you get out of it? I know—your self-love is caressed and your revenge is satisfied. Evidently you need quite a lot of both things. So do I usually, but when I love a person I can do what you don't—put myself aside."

No one told her truths about herself as Walter did. She knew she savored revenge—knew that it came from her sense of being less than a wife to Walter just as she had been found deficient in sorority rushing, and even in her family.

Fran felt her longing for him sweep over her. Keeping his hand gripped in hers, moving closer, she said, "I will put myself aside. I told you that when I came to Italy I would give you back that time in our lives that you say I stole from us in America. But not in Rome—I want to be with you someplace else. If I go to Gran Sasso, it's only for material for the newspaper articles I'm writing. The articles help me stay here. And I think you know why I'm here at all."

They sat there quietly for a long while, watching other people pass.

"Yes, you are right," he said finally. "You should go to Gran Sasso with any guy you want. I am ten times a wooden forester if I don't know that. What bothers me most is that you are a cat with green eyes and that cattish part of you will never be over. Probably it's better this way, otherwise I don't know what could keep me so tied to you."

He drew his hand out of hers and took a package of *Nazionale* cigarettes out of his pocket and lit one, ducking his head between his hands and drawing deeply. He stood up, looked about him searchingly, and smiling down at Fran offered her his hand. "Come on, you cat. Let's go to the nearest *Tabacchi* and play the lottery. Then when I've won a few million lire I'll take you to see Italy -you won't need anyone else."

She stood up and the chestnut shells from her lap fell to the ground at the base of the statue. "You're not just a forester," she told him, "you're Methuselah, too. We've got time. We're just at the beginning."

They walked off into the growing, lengthening shadows of late afternoon among the pines of Villa Borghese.

Bridge. A bridge game with Walter... in Rome. Fran who had played bridge all through college, had thought graduation would signal an end to it. Now it was taking a new turn in her life.

Walter was arranging to have her escorted by a friend of his to the apartment of a certain Pierluigi who held a job at the Ministry but who was conspicuously and mysteriously much better off than his colleagues. Walter sometimes mentioned Pierluigi to Fran; he was believed to have dealings in the black market since it obviously wasn't animal husbandry that paid for his wife's jewels, the liquor, and the smart apartment where he entertained his friends at bridge every few weeks.

It was the first time Walter included Fran in any part of his personal life and though she didn't understand why he would do so, she knew why she accepted. She wanted to see Lucia.

Walter's wife was slight, dark-haired and dark-eyed, and not much older than Fran. She spoke in a curiously gravely and breathy voice and smiled a lot. She was sitting with the other wives and Fran was introduced to them all at once. All were smartly dressed and Lucia, in black, was especially notable for a long string of colored beads which hung almost to her knees and lent her a sense of style and difference. She played with them continuously, fingering them, winding them around her neck and then undoing them, sucking them and knotting them. Fran was immediately certain of what the professor had said: Cassius was satisfied in bed. He had no reason, as he might have had in the states, to hurry the situation in Rome.

Fran was also aware that there was nothing about Lucia that she could dislike or disparage; she imagined it was that way for Walter, too. He had never spoken badly of Lucia. He had mentioned her so seldom and so vaguely that it was as if she were a memory of someone he once knew. Fran recalled his saying: "She is nice

69

enough. Dark hair, like you. But she is a kitten, not a cat. Both can hurt the poor mouse, but while the kitten doesn't know that she is hurting, the cat does know. And she is happy in knowing this. In any case, I like cats better than kittens."

Another time they had walked the Corso and stopped to look in the windows of *Rinascente*, a small department store whose display windows were full of fashion dummies. Walter had laughingly pointed out to Fran a dummy with a long-suffering air who supported on her shoulders a cascade of red fox furs. "Look at them hanging there like a bunch of grapes—what do you think of them? They cost five thousand five hundred lire—not even nine dollars."

"They're terrible," she answered with a grimace. "Who would want such things?"

"Lucia would like some furs," he said pensively, "some good ones."

"That's crazy!"

"Yes, I know, I have no more money than a goldfish. But don't tell me I'm crazy. I know I can give her so little that it would be a real pity if I had to miss the chance to make her happy, especially when this can be done with a fur and not in some other way. If I ever have the money, I will buy her a fur."

His words had touched Fran even as there seemed something suspect in them. Italian women of Lucia's class were spoiled with comforts and tokens of prestige because their husbands were the way they were, and the wives knew it and accepted their tribute of furs and other goods in the tacit trade-off.

Aside from the beads and the rawness of her voice, there was nothing more for Fran to remember about Lucia. She had the kind of low-keyed attributes that made for good wifely qualities in a woman and that men want in their wives, but not necessarily in other women. Lucia was attractive enough, but not enticing; if she wondered about Fran's being there, she showed nothing.

Fran was there to play bridge, a man's game in Italy. While Fran played, Lucia and the other women sat apart talking of their dressmakers and domestic matters. Fran's game was off—she did not play the bold, aggressive game that bridge is for Italian men, but they were patient with her and taught her to bid in Italian. Fran and her escort sat at a table with Walter and his partner and as the evening progressed she became first surprised and then disturbed at the casualness and familiarity of Walter's manner towards her in the presence of the others; he seemed to be hinting at something between them. Fran had supposed that secrecy was vital to him. It had never occurred to her that he might want to show her off, like a kind of trophy from his visit to America, to a gathering of friends. And though the women seemed not to be paying attention to Walter's intimations, the men understood only too well. Walter finessed words as skillfully as cards.

Fran assured herself, as she played her hands, that she would never have continued with Walter if she believed she were just another number to be added to his list. The perseverance and tone of his letters to her when they were thousands of miles apart had convinced Fran of his being in earnest. If only seduction had mattered, everything would have been finished by now. Except that she was coming to realize—that is, the professor had pushed her to realize—that the long wait is the surest arm of seduction.

From her place at the bridge table, Fran glanced occasionally at Lucia among the women sitting on divans and drinking liqueurs, eating chocolates. She was not jealous of her as a person, only as Walter's wife.

"You are playing bridge like a real American tonight," Walter said to her in English, shaking his head in mock dismay when they were partners and she had bid and gone down. "I have seen you play better games—not bridge, necessarily. Perhaps you're nervous now because you're vulnerable."

"Yes, I am vulnerable—more than you, I should say. That's why I play more cautiously and you play in another way, taking risks."

"What are you saying... what are you saying?" boomed Pierluigi in his big voice. "Speak Italian! Or we'll think there's some cheating going on between you partners."

"No cheating, only a question about a bid," Walter said.

"Yes, but a bid for what?"

The men laughed and Walter joined them. Discouraged by her bad playing and feeling cheapened by Walter's innuendoes about her in front of his friends, Fran decided then she would go to Gran Sasso with Professor Balestrini.

When she set out for a travel agency near Piazza Venezia for information about Gran Sasso she hadn't realized it was the day of film star Tyrone Power's wedding to Linda Christian, a minor actress, in the church of Santa Francesca Romana.

Thousands of people were blocking the broad avenue of the Imperial Forums from Piazza Venezia, where Mussolini used to appear on a balcony to harangue the crowds, all the way to the Coliseum. Instead of crying *Duce! Duce!* as Fran remembered seeing the Romans in The March of Time movie newsreels, the crowds of people were now calling *Ty, il bel Ty, Ty il magnifico.* She let herself be carried along with the throngs to a place opposite the Roman Forum where police were trying to clear the avenue.

Perhaps, thought Fran, it was the final dissolution of Fascist sobriety and war privations that induced all Rome to go berserk and throng the streets of its monumental past just to witness the marriage of an American actor to an ambitious starlet. At first Fran wondered if the spectacle had been geared up by Hollywood publicists. But she could sense that the crowd's interest and merriment was genuine and real.

Despite Ty's press statements that he wanted a quiet, dignified ceremony, his bride has chosen as the site of the marriage a church built on the ruins of a temple to Venus which stood in one of the most dramatic settings of Rome—overlooking the Forum and facing the Palatine. Only St. Peter's itself would have been more accessible to crowds. The route to the church of Santa Francesca Romana was Rome's broadest avenue, the one used for military parades, the one most easily packed with spectators.

It was larger than a political demonstration and more good-natured. It was a fine day, bright with sun and Fran sat on an incline opposite the church where the nuptials were going on. Around her vendors were selling balloons, *torrone*, special editions giving the bride's measurements and details of the groom's previous marriage and divorce, along with notes on the trousseau and a prognosis of how long the honeymoon would last. The Romans sprawled along the walls of the Forum, some visible even in the upper tiers of the Coliseum, others darting in and out of the columns of Venus' temple as they dodged the mounted guards and waited for the wedding party to emerge. Good natured gossip and ribald estimates of how Ty would perform were to be heard.

Everyone was there: children who should have been in school, men who should have been at jobs, women who should have been marketing. Mothers took their young to squat in the bushes when necessary; other women scaled walls for closer views and all booed the guards in capes with swords at their sides, who were pushing people away from the barriers near the church where a movie camera had been put in place.

Finally a limousine drove away with the American ambassador inside; then another with Italian dignitaries. The ceremony was over and a great roar came from the crowds as, in other times, happened when a Christian was downed in the Coliseum and shaken in the jaws of a beast.

Moving in slow solemnity, the royal pace, the limousine with the bridal couple advanced. Against a cloud of white tulle, a dark handsome man, his elegant profile visible to all, leaned a little forward and waved. "*Ty! Magnifico!*" shouted a big buxom woman next to Fran and others took up the cry. A great mass of people surged toward the car as if to stop it, but the *carabinieri* stood firm and made an opening for the limousines to get through.

As the crowd dispersed and the reality returned, Fran overheard a man say to his companion, "You see how the Marshall Plan works—America sends us not only bread but even the actors for the circuses."

That evening Fran went to her Italian class. Crossing the big square of San Silvestro where bus lines converged in front of the main post office, she made her way past the parliament building of Montecitorio to the narrow street of Via della Guglia.

She entered the large, cold room lit inadequately by a bulb that hung nakedly from a long cord from the ceiling over the table around which the professor and students met. There was a blackboard on a wall in the darkest part of the room that was never used, but no other furnishings. A few people were at the table; they had their books and were monotonously droning verb endings.

She heard the professor's clipped walk down the corridor, so precise, so regular. He appeared, in his black coat and hat, his books tucked under his arm and with a slight bow said to all of them, *Buona sera*. He kept his coat on as did the others for it was as cold in the room as outside. Taking his place at the head of the table he formally began the lesson.

Occasionally he got up and went alongside a student, jotting a correction in a notebook; once he leaned over Fran's shoulder and wrote, underlining it emphatically, the correct endings for verbs she had gotten wrong. She wondered what he was thinking as he leaned over and his arm brushed her. He said, "*Prego, signorina*, this is the way it goes. Learn it for tomorrow."

In the light of the naked bulb the professor's face seemed stretched tauter, his scars deeper, his eyes more faded that she remembered. And his words were cold and distinct, like the cracking of a whip in the dim room. Fran wondered if she were imagining him more severe than usual. Had he always been so, even prior to their night at St. Peter's, before she bothered to notice him? She was looking about at the others to see if they were noticing anything when he asked her a question. She turned to him blankly, not having understood anything but her name.

Balestrini was frowning impatiently. "Your mind is evidently on *carnevale, signorina* and not on verbs!"

"No, *professore*," she said, "on skiing."

He raised his brows in surprise at her answer. He had decided not to pursue her. There would be other students or secretaries, as there had been in the past—little affairs that functioned smoothly without tangling him up and creating complications. After the evening in her room, the American had seemed too complicated, and he too weary.

Yet here she was again in his class, smiling and charming and attractive. The proverb said one always fishes best in troubled waters. So if she were troubled by Cassius, her loneliness, and now his own advances, so much the better for him. She seemed to be trying to sort things out like chunks of pure black shadows there, pure bright light here. This was the time he told himself.

Perhaps she had thought over his idea and had re-considered. Had she just made it plain that she would go to Gran Sasso with him? Balestrini found himself excited at the prospect. He was impatient for the lesson to end. Going through his professorial paces, he frowned at the other students and their lesson books which kept him occupied. Even when the hour was over, some still surrounded him with their little problems of past participles or subjunctive mood. But, as he hurried the explanations, he noticed that Signorina Molletone lingered in the classroom, not leaving.

They were finally alone. He came over and said, "So you have decided for Gran Sasso, after all. I think you are right. And I am glad."

"I am glad, too," Fran said.

He took her hand gently in his. "Now that we are both here alone for once, I should like to give you a rather different kind of lesson. Not verbs. Poetry."

"Baudelaire?"

"No." He opened a book and asked, "Do you know Montale?"

She shook her head.

"A very big poet. Our best now. I want to read you his "Portovenere".

Fran smiled at the man who had a poem for every occasion, who steered his life through the emotions of others. He read her the short verse and the sounds were soothing -the soft, malleable Italian rippled like waves lapping at a shore. It was a gentle lulling; she was receptive to the cadence and rhythm of the verse and did not strain to catch the meaning.

When he finished he looked at her inquisitively.

"I was listening to the sounds—I didn't get all the words."

"I'll read it again in Italian and then translate it."

"*Come una fanciulletta amica,*" she heard. Like a young girl, a friend. The words were so pliant, mobile. They came without effort and meant something young and soft and tender.

He finished and looked at her.

"Beautiful," she said.

"Listen, I'll translate:

> Triton emerges there
> from waves that wash
> the threshold of a Christian
> temple, and each new hour
> is ancient. Each doubt
> is led by the hand
> as you lead a young girl,
> your friend.

> There it is not important
> to see yourself
> or stand still to hear yourself.
> There you are at the origins
> and decision is foolish:
> you will leave later
> to assume a visage.

Balestrini looked up from his book. "There it is. That is Portovenere—a lovely sea town in Liguria, you should see it someday. But the poem is more—it is something of all of us. What do you think?"

"I am not sure," Fran said slowly, "why he says decision is foolish. Decision can be so much else—painful, hard, necessary." She stretched her hands out in a gesture of confusion. "Decision can be almost anything, but I don't think having to make one is foolish."

"I know what you mean. In our own little lives, our circumscribed worlds, decision for each of us is something big, important. But here, you see, Montale says we are in the presence of both pagan antiquity and Christian endurance, of waves that will continue to wash that shore long after you and I and our decisions are gone. Here, as he says, we are at the origins."

Balestrini's voice grew more animated as he spoke and gestured repeatedly. "This is the beauty of the poem—to show the futility of intellectual inversion before what is natural and ancient and inevitable in the large scheme of things. In such moments and in such presence it is useless to go on looking inward at yourself, to stop to listen to yourself—your doubts, your conflicts, your limitations. In certain times and places it is foolish to decide. Later you put on the mask that you will present, for custom's sake, to an indifferent world."

Balestrini paused and looked at her. "You must have known at sometime that one moment of grace when the doubts which seemed so heavy just loosen from you and slide away. You can dispel them as gently as you lead by the hand a child. Or as I would lead the young girl who is my friend."

He took her hand in his. "Do you know what I mean?"

"Yes."

Yes, she said to herself. I know and I'm glad. It was as if she felt in that moment the grace of which he had spoken. She had somewhat divined it on her arrival in Rome—the futility of rationalizing and planning, trying to program and control things. But now she felt it in its entirety and all the pragmatism of her American education seemed to slip from her like a loosened wrapper. Here, yes, she felt at the origin of things, and even of herself. And why renounce a moment of grace? Later, yes, later she might have to assume the mask. But now? now she was here and she felt the foolishness of her doubts.

Balestrini bent over and kissed her hand, his lips faintly brushing her skin. "I am sorry about the other night," he said. "I was boorish. Please forgive me."

"I didn't understand why you were so angry when you left."

"And so clumsy. But never mind. We will go to Gran Sasso this Friday. And don't worry, nothing will happen there that you don't want to happen. You will ski, you will see the Abruzzi and write a fine article."

He smiled benevolently.

"What arrangements are there to make?"

"We don't have to worry about rooms—there are always plenty at this season. I'll get the bus seats. All you have to do is be at Piazza Esedra on Friday at two o'clock. Can you get there with your skis?— it wouldn't be so wise for me to come to get you."

"Yes, I can be there—the porter will call me a taxi. But will we get there the same night if we start so late?"

"I have a morning appointment on Friday," he said. "We'll get as far as Aquila that night and stay there. We'll be at Campo Imperatore early the next morning, then back in Rome by Monday evening. And now, God bless our English friends for giving us this time alone tonight!"

"Would they have if they had known the explanation was assignations and not verbs?"

"Tomorrow in class we'll have verbs again and I'll call you *signorina* and I shall be stern if you are day-dreaming again and not listening. But don't mind. Just wait for me at the bus stop and I'll come and say something nice just to show I haven't changed. Now let's go to the bar and get some hot punch, it's cold as hell in here!"

"As hell?"

"Yes, hell," said Balestrini decisively as he turned out the light. "The ninth circle."

Fran was thinking of another circle—the one where Paolo and Francesca (her namesake) were borne continuously on the current of their love, stuck forever together and moved by their passion in unrelenting circles, without stop, forever.

She went through the motions of preparing to meet Balestrini like a sleep-walker. A cloud of complacency enveloped her: everything seemed to be on a track of its own without her volition.

She had walked in her sleep as a child. From the dark, dreamless continent of sleep she'd rise and wander as if not already in her home but seeking it, walking through the strange unsettling territory of the still house, her disquietude violating the sense of deep quiet and repose that night signified in tranquil lives. Upsetting her parents, it confirmed what they thought—that she was odd in everything, even sleep.

Much, too, of her early waking life was like that of a sleepwalker—unsubstantial, seen and experienced through layers of foggy unreality. They thought she was withdrawn because of shyness. She lived in a bubble of unreal containment. All she knew, in fact, was to take the step away from what she didn't fit into. One step, then another. An opposite direction.

Going to Piazza Esedra Fran felt she might have been going off anywhere, with anyone. It made not the slightest difference.

Settled on the bus to Aquila, Balestrini would say at intervals, "Are you comfortable? Would you like to smoke?". At first she just sat back and looked out at what passed before her eyes with deep wonder, as if the landscape she watched so closely were the image of her soul and the knowledge of it both strange and essential to her. She was silent, as if she were alone, immersed in her thoughts.

They sped past blossoming groves—magenta blooms on almond trees, white on apple trees. The country earth was in resurgence with the spring of late February. Olive trees were silver green against the blue sky. Towns crowned the hills and seemed to grow out of the very rock they perched on, hanging from steep heights or nestled in valleys.

"Just like the towns on the papier-mâché tunnels of an electric train set," Fran said, remembering her brothers' trains, set up each Christmas.

"Yes. I think all Italy must be like a child's set for Americans or Australians who come from such large lands. We're all packed and crammed into a place no bigger than your Florida. Here you can never be far from a settlement—everywhere there's the sign of man and his works. Look at that town—how it hangs there! It is there so charmingly because Italy is poor and has had to carve habitations out of rock for her too many people. America is large, rich, abundant."

"*Semper surfeit* is our motto!" It occured to her that size made a fundamental difference in the way the people of the two countries behaved—there was the tight cohesiveness of Italy with a habitation around every bend, and a great central piazza in every town that allowed people to come together in human exchange, whereas America separated them by the great spaces of its landscape.

Amused at her outburst, Balestrini said lightly, "I didn't know you held such strong sentiments about your country."

"*This* is my country, too. My grandparents all came from Italy. Now I have found my way back."

"Yes, I suppose we should all find our way back—if not in physical space, at least in time. But most Americans don't care, do they? They are so well off that I suppose they would rather not see the uncomfortable places many of them came from."

"Yes. My family thinks I'm crazy to be here. Italy was kept out of lives. But once I got past the guards, and out of the cage the place outside was better than I could have ever imagined!"

"But my dear," said Balestrini with exaggerated and teasing concern, "what kind of life did you have over there to compare it with a cage?"

"Comfortable and confining," she said. "I didn't know anything of importance. I studied and did well in college but I didn't know what my studies were for, or how to be popular, how to participate in groups, or make friends. I didn't know how to speak to my grandparents, or how to be curious about them as human beings. I knew next to nothing about the war, the WPA, American political parties, the extermination of the Jews in Europe, or even how babies are born. I was educated and ignorant."

"That's quite a statement—a courageous one, in fact. It means you see your past limitations and can turn them around."

"*Magari!* What a nice Italian word that is—you just send it out and let it make your wishes come true."

"And we here in Italy, under fascism, were lusting for America, its freedom to speak out. It was our Elysian Fields, the best of all possible countries in this imperfect world."

"Yes, maybe the best so far in an imperfect world."

"You will go back eventually, won't you?"

Fran frowned and looked out. "I suppose. But I will be better for having been here."

"Yes," he said after a pause. "Better or worse."

"That's the chance—at least it won't be the same."

"That's important," he said and they fell silent. He thought of his own unchanging life: lectures at the University, a few critical pieces or translations to publish in literary magazines, and tutorial sessions with foreigners four nights a week to make ends meet. Marisa went to the dressmaker and played canasta; his father dozed in a chair near the window; his son was a fatuous bore who talked of his vocation for the priesthood. And he, Gregorio Balestrini, who had in his youth written poetry, felt not yet old, but no longer young. He was somewhere between ages, as Fran was between worlds.

As the bus hurtled through villages, Fran saw loungers hanging about the town portals with an air of such picturesqueness she imagined an all-seeing Italian Tourist Board placing them there for the effect. Women balanced spitoon-like jugs on their heads and wore black stockings and thick boots. There was an exuberance of spring in all the country outside Rome and the sky was brilliant cerulean with great chunks of cumulus clouds floating through it. Tawny and rose-colored farmhouses huddled at regular intervals in the dips and crooks of hills. And, occasionally, in country villages where the bus stopped to pick up a passenger, girls would approach the windows and shyly offer eggs, one in each hand, for sale. One elderly lady, surrounded by parcels and bags, bought an egg, punctured it with her hat pin and drank it down in one swift act. As Fran gasped, the professor leaned closer and whispered, "It gives great energy."

When they arrived in Rieti for a ten-minute stopover, the last market wagons and push-carts filled with thick mountain boots, kitchen utensils, cheeses, sausages, and underwear, still lined the piazza. Everyone left the bus for coffee at the nearest bar. When they re-boarded, they were joined by a few black-stockinged peasant women with bicycles who paid only to ride uphill, getting out before the descent to coast the rest of the way home.

The bus climbed up and up, twisting and turning through stone villages and past fields of snow or barren stretches of brown. Once in a while they saw a few goats, or some sullen people who stared at the speeding bus; occasionally they'd see on the white-washed wall of a farmhouse the fading letters of a fascist slogan: *Il fascista disdegna la vita comoda* (A fascist scorns the easy life) that seemed, in that inhospitable environment a cruel irony.

Fran made note of it for some future use.

"All Italy used to be infested with those indecencies," Balestrini told her. "In places of indescribable squalor you'd see 'Better to live one day as a lion than a hundred years as a sheep'....'Order and Discipline'... 'Rome Dominates'... Mussolini is always Right.' All those slogans were on walls, barns, houses, post-offices. Of course, after the war everyone rushed around with pails of whitewash to cancel the Duce's words, but no one seems to have gotten this far yet. And maybe they never will. It doesn't matter. These people never changed their ways for slogans on a wall. Except, of course, Ovid."

"Was he from here?"

"Yes, Sulmona. The most lascivious and sophisticated poet of Rome's decadence is from this stern, puritanical Abruzzi. There's the triumph of mind over matter!"

"Now I suppose you will be reading Ovid at Gran Sasso!" Fran was irritated by his constant literariness. But Balestrini took it as a joke between them and laughed.

"We don't need poets anymore. When we are like this, we are the poets. And it's better."

As they went further into the Abruzzi the land changed from spring-filled valleys to a desolate stretch of boulder-strewn hills. There was a rugged appeal to these high reaches—the chiseled looking people, the winds, the rocks all spoke of endurance. With the setting of the sun, the hills seemed blood-soaked and above them chunks of white cloud changed to wisps of orange and pink until they finally faded into the blue and purple night. It was dark when they got to Aquila.

Aquila—the eagle; the brooding, cold air of the town and its asperity reminded Fran of her aloof and austere Latin teacher from the Convent School, Sister Aquiline. And the Abruzzi reminded her of Mr. di Tomasi who had come from the region. At the hotel desk, she chose a postcard to send to him and wrote: *Saluti da Ovidio e da me.*

In a deserted, cobble-stoned street Balestrini and Fran found a trattoria of the type called *caratteristico* for the regional pictureque-ness it exuded. Majolica plates decorated the ceiling and a tree grew into the room through a hole in the exterior wall. When a huge corner clock struck the hour, it played *La donna è mobile.*

"I love this place," Fran said warmly, as Balestrini knew she would. "I'm glad we got out of that empty hotel."

"*Che melanchonia!*" he replied in hearty agreement. "We seem to be the only ones there except for the disagreeable clerk and he'd probably leave, too, if he could. But you see, I told you we would have no trouble about rooms."

Fran knew he was baiting her. Registering, the desk clerk had asked, *Camera matrimoniale?* and there had been the briefest pause before Balestrini answered, no, two single rooms. She smiled faintly and Balestrini said, "And if it's cold tonight and that hotel, as I suspect, is not heated, you may be sorry that we don't have the double bed that sour clerk wanted to give us."

"Let's drink to keep warm," she rejoined. And they did, choosing the red wine of the region, a strong one with as robust and unyielding a quality as the land which produced it. Balestrini ordered for them—*spaghetti alla matriciana* and then a speciality of the region, boar cooked *alla salamòia* in a sauce of herbs, wine, cloves and the acerbic local vinegar, which was highly prized.

"This is a tough place," Fran said when a leathery-faced countryman dressed all in black with a great mantle slung about him came into the restaurant. "Just look at the people... they look like what they eat, boar with vinegar! And yet every bit of space is inhabited or worked or used in some way. In America there are still wildernesses. I suppose in Italy there is no virgin land by now."

"There is nothing virgin in Italy," said Balestrini, "land or otherwise. This is a country rich only in its non-virginity."

Fran tilted her head appraising his banter, and decided to return it. "We do have a cult of virginity in America—the great virgin lands waiting for the plow or big business to break them; virgin resources never before tapped; one hundred per-cent virgin wool guaranteed by Good Housekeeping magazine." She laughed and fingered her wine glass, holding it to the light. "I worked in an advertising office and wrote copy once for a virgin aluminum pan."

Balestrini was watching her with his habitual smile of amused skepticism. She took another sip of the astringent wine and leaned back in her chair gazing at the plates that clung so crazily to the ceiling.

"In the ad I left out the word virgin and my copy chief told me to do it over because the most important part about the pan was not its capacity or usefulness but that it was virgin aluminum. He taught me that even the virginity of a pan is important."

"Maybe so in pans, but not, thank God in people. Celibate or not, no human stays virgin because life itself is the raper. Just living uses us. So, to be or not to be—a pan or alive. The choice is yours. Now what do you choose to finish up this mountain meal?"

Fran sighed deeply and shook her head. "You choose."

"Then we'll have their pecorino cheese, walnuts, and more wine."

"Good!" she said, happy and warmed with the wine, with the plates looking down at her, and with Balestrini to talk to. Feeling giddy, she said idly, "No virgins in Italy?....did you court your wife with love poetry and make love to her before you married?"

"Good Lord, no!" He looked shocked."Are you mad? For the two years I courted her all I was allowed was to kiss her on the cheek—not even the lips! For two years I desired her so much it was like a constant fever. I didn't dare read poetry to her, only to myself, thinking of her. She was a student, like you, when I met her... she was young, like you. But it's all past history now."

Fran thought of desire held back. Would she, as Balestrini, once satisfied, become indifferent because it was the tension of wanting someone not the fulfillment that had held the interest?

"But you said you loved her in the beginning," she continued. "Why wouldn't you read poetry to her, kiss her, make love?"

"I couldn't do that to the girl I was going to marry," Balestrini said sternly, his look very severe and formal. "She's from a good family, she wasn't just anybody. She was going to be my wife and I had to wait."

"I find that not only priggish, but vulgar -men looking at women in terms of an undefiled acquisition." She looked at him skeptically, her mind reeling with her thoughts and with the effect of the wine. "Such a sham. Marriage, I mean. That two-year reverence for her virginity was in terms of her market value."

Balestrini looked at her in utter surprise and she, too, was surprised at what she had said. What did it matter to her that this formal professor had married his wife for her chastity and good family and then found he had no love for her, nor anything in common with her, only a lifetime together to be gotten through? And yet it did matter.

She was discovering that Walter and Balestrini were both the same man; both had married not for love but out of a deliberately created desire. And once that had been satisfied, the rest was emptiness. Then had begun the infidelities, and the assurance with each new woman that she brought him more than his wife did. An endless procession over the years. With Walter it would be the same. Why hadn't he told her at Thanksgiving that he was not free? "The wine has loosened your tongue," Balestrini was saying as he poured more into her glass. "In any case, let's just say it doesn't matter if you free yourself from virginity with marriage or without it. That's the point—you don't *lose* virginity, you free yourself from it! And with that comes freedom from the kind of self-love which is the biggest sin of all."

"Well, maybe. But it's frightening, just the same, to lose your separateness and merge with someone else. Isn't that what the Church knows, and why it insists on celibacy? To concentrate the self rather than disperse it?"

"Every human interaction is a risk. As you said before about going back to America, nothing can be the same again and that's the chance that's taken."

They were alone now in the restaurant and as the clock chimed once more its tinny strains of Rigoletto, Balestrini raised his voice above them. "It is infinitely better to love too many—though how, in God's name, can there be too much love around?—than to go on preserving self-love with the sanctimonious feeling that it's a virtue to be stingy with it."

"Love—what is love," Fran murmured drowsily, tired from the trip, the wine, the talk.

"Think of what Dante said: *Amor, ch'a nullo amato amar perdona.* Offered, it can't be refused."

In the drab, ill-lighted hotel they paused in the hall and Balestrini unlocked Fran's door. "Thank goodness," she said, throwing off her coat and flinging herself down on the bed. Balestrini bent down to kiss her. "Good night," he said and started to go.

"Don't go. Stay with me, here," she said. She had drunk too much but even so some clinical, undrowsy, un-wined part of herself was saying, Let this be done; let me give up self-love. She closed her eyes. Balestrini murmured to her as if from some distance. She felt his hands and lips as if through a screen of silk—the gentle silk of wine and sleepiness. She felt clothes being removed. There was the shock of his flesh against hers. In the cold of that still hotel she felt the warm attachment of their flesh. But nothing else. And when Balestrini was still, lying beside her, she thought, he has made love to me and he has felt something but I have not.

He slept, she was awake; the night was black nothingness around them and slowly she succumbed to it. She woke with the light of dawn, dressed quietly and went to the window. She watched the gray day come into the gray town disclosing the cold stone buildings from the shadows of the receding night.

When she heard the phone ring next door in Balestrini's room, she looked at her watch: six-thirty, the time he had asked to be called. She went over to the bed and unexpectedly as she leaned to touch his shoulder, a great sadness filled her so that tears came again to her eyes. She wiped them away, touched his shoulder gently until he was awake.

He sat up, startled, looking around him as if trying to recall where he was. "Are you awake already? What time is it?"

Fran stood there; both the wine-induced suppleness of the night and the subsequent remorse were gone and she felt only conventionally awkward, in a social situation whose rules she didn't know. What does one say to a lover? How does one act? Resolutely she sat down on the edge of the bed and, with affectionate politeness, smiled at him and waited.

He leaned over, touseled her hair, and said, "How are you?"

He felt rested and well and told himself that though she had not responded, it was no matter—they never do the first time. Now there would be other times. Love was easy for him, an old and comfortable friend.

The telephone was still ringing in the next room.

She jumped up from the bed, glad of its insistence, and searching in his coat pocket for his room key, said, "I'll get it!" The tender look on his face disturbed her. She didn't want him to have those feelings for her. Whatever else there would be between them, she didn't want it to be love.

In the undisturbed order of Balestrini's room Fran picked up the telephone receiver, heard the desk clerk announce the time, and hung up without speaking. She lay down on the untouched bed and stared at the ceiling.

What offended her the most, she thought, was the dispassionate way in which she handled her emotions. She felt like a bespectacled, old file clerk who had tidied her desk and put everything in order before finally locking the drawer that contained her private stuff: and what was the treasure she so carefully locked up?—an almost empty tube of lipstick, a bunch of letters, a photo, a smeared kleenex. Fran felt that the emotions, which she kept so locked up as her private treasure, were just as banal.

Balestrini had dressed and came back to his room for his shaving gear. Silently she watched him shave. Full of good spirits, he came over and holding her head gently, kissed her forehead and cheeks. "Don't worry," he said, "everything is fine."

Crossing The Alps

The hotel at Campo Imperatore was a strange affair, its front a convex bulge which resembled the bow of a ship. They had reached it by funicular from the station where the bus line terminated and the Gran Sasso mountain range began. The funicular ascended the mountain perpendicularly past rough crags and snow and forest. Swung out into space in the tiny cable car, Fran felt literally lifted away from the world. Half-way up they changed cable-cars. The landing at the top was connected to the hotel through a long tunnel whose shadowy interior was pierced at intervals by candles, and through which came the far-off echo of voices.

It was built in the Fascist-modern style of the thirties and had rapidly become out-dated; it had the air of shabbiness and defeat that so many unmistakable Fascist era post-offices and railroad stations carried with them, almost all of them painted the same raw red that, with time and neglect, turned to the rusty color the hotel now was.

Fran slept the remainder of the morning and it wasn't until after lunch that she accompanied Balestrini on a walk in the vast white stillness around the hotel. The sky was intensely blue as it is at the seashore in July and there was nothing in the all white expanse except them and silence. The air was sharp and clear, the quiet deep. Fran's spirit lifted at the gorgeous ruggedness of the mountain peaks, the snowy vistas, scrubby trees, crevices, and clouds breaking over nearby crags.

Later she joined a ski group with two young men and an older one who were going out with the ski master, *il maestro*. He led them cross country to a mild run of a few kilometers called *La Scenderella*. At the top of it they passed briefly through clouds, seeming to totter on the edge of nothing. Their *maestro*, a blustery tanned mountain man, started yodeling and slaloming and they followed him on a run between high banks of snow that left them breathless and exhilarated at the end, not far from the second funicular which took them back to the top. Fran's cheeks were red and glowing from the spray of snow and cold air, and she felt joyous. They did the run until the shadows of late afternoon fell over the snow.

From her monastic-like room Fran called through the connecting door, "I love it here, Gori! I never imagined it would be so wonderful—I've never done skiing like this before—at home, it was just little hills called drumlins—here, it's like flying!"

"Good," he said, coming into her room and hugging her, "from now on whenever you ski, you will remember being here with me." He kissed her, then drew back and scrutinized here. "Your face is sun-burned, you know. Be careful tomorrow, but tonight it is wonderful. It makes your eyes as bright as aquamarines—wonderful eyes! Let's go down to the bar and drink to your eyes and the way they are looking at me in this moment."

"First I'm taking some of these things off," she said, guiding him out of her room and closing the door between them. She took off her boots and ski pants and heavy sweaters and lay across her bed. It had been a perfect day. Contentment itself turned to remorse as she thought of Walter. He would be someplace at a Carnevale party, dancing with Lucia, flirting with her friends—probably not even mindful that Fran had gone away. She got up impatiently, dressed, and knocked on Balestrini's door. "Let's get a drink," she said.

The ski-master was at the bar, shooting dice with the barman. "Ah, *brava, signorina*," he waved to Fran when she entered with Balestrini. "You did pretty well today, now have some *petrolio* to oil up your joints."

The barman, Arturo, poured two drinks of clear, thickish Doppio Kummel liqueur for her and the professor. An old rendition of Stormy Weather blared on the phonograph and outside there was darkness and snow and silence.

"Were you in this area when the Germans came in and took out Mussolini?" Balestrini asked Arturo.

"Right here! in this very hotel—first when they brought Il Duce here on the little king's orders in July of '43, and then when the

Germans rescued him in September."

"Yes," Balestrini mused. "That was when the Allies landed in Sicily, and then all the Ministers got together and gave Mussolini a vote of no confidence."

"Those Germans moved like they'd been rehearsing it for years. They sent paratroopers in to surround the hotel. Then they hurried Il Duce off to a helicopter which had landed up above on a stone ridge. I saw his face as they rushed him out—unshaven, a bitter man. They had him wear a hat down over his eyes and he looked like those gangsters in American films."

Fran thought of the fascist dictator lodged up there, alone in captivity and defeat among the stones and pasturing goats... in an empty hotel with no populace to bluster at; he could thrust out his jaw and clench his fist all he liked but there were only rocks and wind up there to return the salute.

"Yes, he looked like a lost soul," Arturo said, "a whipped dog. It wasn't even possible to hate him at that moment, despite all the bad he had done. It wasn't yet cold when the Germans came for him, but they wrapped him in a dark overcoat with the collar turned up. No more uniforms—he was like an ordinary frightened man any-where. And those Germans! they stood there grinning and talking and I said to myself, if I were Il Duce I'd rather stay on the moun-tain with the goats than be rescued by the likes of them. But he had no choice at that point he wasn't boss in the country anymore, *they* were. And *we* had no choice, either! We had both armies fighting us in our land—the Allies and the Germans. It's funny, you know. All Italy was convinced that with Mussolini out, peace would descend on us -after all, it was his war—no one else wanted it. What we forgot was that we had to pay for having had a Mussolini for twenty years."

"Those must have been bad times," said Fran.

"Yes, they were bad. The English and Americans fighting up from the south, the Germans in the north deporting us. We were caught between them like imbeciles wondering why good times hadn't dropped from heaven like a visit of the Madonna! When we finally learned to fight for peace, we did it better than we ever did the war."

Fran pictured Walter fighting as a partisan against the fascists; and she thought of her father who had been conflicted in his loyalties by being both an American First patriot and still hoping that somehow Mussolini would prevail over the English and French and carry Italy to glory. Yes, secretly he would have liked a triumphant Italy. She remembered a repellent scene with a visiting uncle who lorded it over them because he was Canadian. In a moment of unaccountable rage, food dribbling from his mouth in his haste to speak, he accusingly asked the room why the Italians lost the war—why were they such cowards, why didn't they fight? They probably didn't want to fight for Fascism, she said. But there was no placating men like her father and uncle who, patriots of the New World though they were, wanted, in their confused loyalties, to be avenged for the slurs against their old world origins.

The hotel dining room was curved like an ellipse with a continuous expanse of windows at one end that looked out, by day, over stretches of snow and at night showed only deep blackness, as if they were in a cave. All the tables were set, but there were only a half-dozen people in the place. Their talk and the clink of their silver and glassware could not dispel the thick black silence which reigned on the far side of the windows, suspending them in an unreality of place and time.

Fran felt herself in some special realm. Her face glowed with color, her eyes were bright. Balestrini, too, had lost his pallor and was smiling and happy from his walks.

"My legs are sore. I don't know how I'll ski tomorrow."

"You'll ski, my dear. I'll give you a rub-down later to relax your muscles and you'll be fine."

She knew he would come to her that night, and the next. She had devised the rationale that being with the professor was preferable to taking a risk with Walter. It was the gloss to her trip, though a glimpse of the hard truth, which lay underneath (her cowardice, her duplicity) came through from time to time. The only answer is wine, she thought. As she reached for the liter bottle of house wine on the table, Balestrini stopped her with his hand over hers.

"Too much of this is bad for skiing," he said genially.

with

"I'm not skiing now," she frowned. And then she blurted out, "You should know that I'm not in love you. I like you, I like being here with you, but...."

Initially taken aback, he recovered himself quickly. He patted her hand soothingly and said blandly, "Don't worry—it's enough for us to be here now. You'll see that everything has been all right between us." Then, changing his tone as their waiter approached the table, he said, "What did you think of Arturo's story?"

Fran looked up, relieved. "I felt sorry for Mussolini in the abstact," she said slowly, "you know, the downfall of the great, being cheered one day and kicked out the next only to end up hanging like a carcass in a butcher shop. But when I think of the war and all those poor villages we passed through, I see him for the bully he was and at what cost to the people he held his power and I despise him. Were you in the war?"

Again surprised, the smile left his face. "*In it?*" he asked. "I was both in it and out of it. There was no one living in Italy, whatever the sentiments, who was not in the war in some way during the Fascist period. But for the part you mean, I was out. I was living in a village in the north, near the Tyrol, when the Allied invasion and worst fighting took place. Are you disappointed? Did you imagine me a hero?"

His tone was light, but there was considerable tension in his face, weighing down the corners of his mouth. He thought of the twenty years spent under Fascism with its illusions of grandeur, its easy bravado and cheap hope of bypassing the present for faith in the future only to find the future continued the mortgaged past. The mirage wears away finally. By then the evil remains, fixed into habit. There had been for twenty years the shameful chain of necessity tying him down, keeping him still. There had been the need of lies, of fawning, of a thousand compromises and subterfuges with himself and with other men. Life had become a system of little deceits and exchanges of favors to keep his teaching post and curry favor. Years without reprieve, without the chance of shouting out: Here I am, this is how I think!—this is who I really am, and what I believe! And though the years of his silence weighed on him and oppressed him, the fighting, when it began, had terrorized him and he had fled to the north, to the village where he and Marisa always spent their summers and he had waited there for two years until the guns and bombs had stopped, until the fighting ceased and it was safe to return to Rome. He had thought it would be easy to take up his life again. Teaching and writing and the peace to do it in was all he ever wanted. But he found the memory of what he had done or not done in those past years still kept him hostage.

Fran noticed the shadow which passed over his face. "We won't talk about the war," she said. But she had seen in those moments the man he was. It was what gave him that look of prim withdrawal, the professorial disdain which was his badge in Rome.

She wondered what it was in people that led them to obey when they knew that the rules and regulations were absurd, or worse. Would she have been brave living under a dictatorship? Would she have broken some of their silly laws that forbade the reading of certain prohibited authors—yes, she might have. She had had no compunction about reading authors on the Index of Prohibited Books when she was at the Convent School. Nor about parking illegally, nor even, if lost and going the wrong way, about making a U-turn where signs were posted against doing so. Those infractions simply seemed to her to be saying that she could think for herself and not be made to follow blindly what was unreasonable. But could such boldness for little infractions be carried through to civil disobedience on the grand scale? Would she actually be able to stand up against the injustices practiced in the fascist regime towards political enemies, or protest the racial laws? Making an illegal U-turn was one thing, putting one's life on the line for ideals was another. She thought that she was not that brave. But neither was she as supine as Balestrini.

And yet she understood the failure of nerve—in college she had shied away from literature which was her love to take the commercial courses which would guarantee her a job because she retained that mentality of lying low and not taking risks which the original peasant immigrants had brought over, along with the ability for hard work to make good materially. It was on that level that the failure of nerve set in; the fear that she was not as good, as learned, as cultured, as worthy as the right people.

Balestrini's good spirits were dissipated and a look of such dejection came over him that Fran was sorry for having judged him. She patted his arm.She could almost be more moved by him than by Walter because she felt Balestrini's need for her in a way that Walter, with his ironies and artfulness, had never revealed. She was on stage with Walter, an ingenue doing her comedy of manners; with Balestrini she felt the bond, despite their separate worlds and stories, of their both having known defeat.

That night he came to her room and as he massaged her legs with a lotion and she felt his strong, expert touch, she said to him, almost apologetically, "Last night... I don't know why... I didn't feel...." It was more than an apology, it was an overture.

He understood. He held her face cupped in his hands. "Soon, very soon, you will feel everything. You look tonight like an Egyptian princess reincarnated." He traced with his finger the arch of her brows above her deep-set and slightly slanted eyes. In the half-light of the hotel room, with the burden of snow and silence encapsulating them, he told her he found in her the warmth of exotic countries—she made him think of a Greek hetaera, a Lydian courtesan, a Sicilian handmaid to the Arab overlords. Her body was white except where it reflected the rosy light of the lamp beside the bed. Her hair was long and he buried his head in it and then searched for her mouth.

They made love that night and she came to life under the urgency of his touch and the great emotion she absorbed from him. He lost his dejection, she her guilt. She knew abandon for the first time. She did not think. She lay tranquil, Balestrini close to her, not letting him go until her arms released him of themselves as she fell into sleep.

She skied the next day and when she stood at the top of the run and looked across the snow-space and felt herself young and strong at the top, capable of going with the wind, she forgot her uncertainties, her fears and doubts about herself—who she was, what she would be. Life at the top of the run was instant, contained in the moment. It was mastering something so intense she was breathless with the joy of it. It was all there, swiftly, in the act, with no before or after. With each run she shed the shell formed by all the perceptions and impasses of her life until then, and flew toward her freedom. The same flight, the same freedom, she felt again in Balestrini's arms at night when they made love.

She understood that how she was with Balestrini, trusting and natural, she could not be with Walter. There was something easy between her and Balestrini because she expected nothing from him; from Walter she wanted everything. And in the cold and lucid air in the highest reaches of the Gran Sasso range, Fran wondered if love would last if she kept seeing Balestrini. Was the best way to love Walter by making love to Balestrini?

Fran left the Abruzzi with a vision of stone and small patches of land cultivated in any crevice; bleak, hard lives were imprinted on her memory -the huddled villages where austere men with folded arms stared after their bus, the stern-faced children chasing goats through rocky fields, the women beating wash in icy streams.

In Rome, the air was almost tepid when Fran and Balestrini kissed goodbye and went their different ways with only their tanned faces and the echo of mountain stillness to remind them of their past sanctuary.

It was *Martedì grasso*—fat Tuesday, the farewell to flesh of a libertine people who understand that an Ash Wednesday is inevitably in the natural flow of things, and so make the most of dispensation. On the first day of March, the last day before the beginning of Lent, Fran lay in bed regarding the daylight which flooded her room and gave brightness and cheer to the props of her life: the typewriter on the desk, the books and bottles, the lean face of Cassius in the painting. And flung into a corner, its time past, her ski garb. Ash Wednesday, she thought, and wondered if she already figuratively wore the cross of ashes on her forehead like a penitent.

Fran was still in bed when Amelia came in for the breakfast tray. "Signor Molletone called while you were gone and asked that you return his call before tonight," she said.

"The young man or the old one?"

Amelia shrugged her shoulders. "The one who lisps and eats his words. He was surprised you had gone skiing."

It was Tino who had called. Now they would expect explanations of where she had been. She hadn't thought of that.

"*Mamma mia*, how red your face is," Amelia was saying. "You've got to be careful—the March sun in Rome can make you mad."

"Why is that?"

"How should I know why, I am not educated. That is what they say: *il sole di marzo, ti fa pazzo*."

"Well, I'm for sun and light, so I'll have to take my chances."

"How the *tramontana* blew while you were gone, *signorina*! They say that when the wind cries like that another soul has gone to hell."

Fran considered Amelia's store of sayings and how they gave direction and substance to her life. People like her smelled the weather far off, they sensed what was in the very air, and set their moods by a glance at the sky. The nights Fran had spent in Balestrini's arms in the calm of the mountains, Amelia had heard the wind shriek of souls gone to hell. Now there was the March sun to make her mad. She laughed and got out of bed.

Amelia picked up the tray. "You're happy today, signorina,—it's *martedi grasso*, time to have fun, that's why you're happy."

"*Si,si*, today I'm happy, tomorrow's another day."

"Tomorrow is ashes," said Amelia, her voice drifting down the hallway as she began a plaintive song.

Tino's wife answered Fran's call. "*Ciao*, Anna, this is Francesca. How are you? The maid here told me Tino called."

Timid by nature, unobtrusive, Anna's voice was uncertain as she asked, "Did you have a good time? The maid said you went skiing."

Confidently, Fran said, "Yes, skiing. I went up to Terminillo for the week-end with the two English ladies who live here. Was there something important Tino had to tell me?"

"Not so important, but we are sorry we don't see you more often and would have liked you to come to dinner this past Sunday. But maybe you can come tonight if it isn't disturbing for you. It's the last night of Carnevale—but maybe you have something to do that is more amusing."

Anna spoke apologetically, sorry not to have anything better to offer. Her own life was one of abnegation and fatigue, but she imagined, without rancor or envy, that the American Molletones led lives of gaiety and amusement. She was not envious of her husband's relative from America. It was all in the scheme of things that Fran be light-hearted and privileged and she not. Their lives were different. That's how it was.

Fran heard the apology in Anna's voice and felt sorry for her. "Of course, I will come, Anna, I will be glad to see you again. What time do you want me?"

"Come early, Francesca," she replied with a happy lilt. "How well you speak Italian now!"

"That's why you haven't seen more of me, Anna. I have Italian lessons usually in the evening. But tonight there is none because of Carnevale."

"Good," Anna said, giving her nervous laugh. Fran could picture her—slight and wiry, a thin plain woman with a prominent nose and lank, permanented hair held off her face with a bobby pin.

On first arriving in Rome, Frances had gone to stay with the Molletone relatives. She liked the old man, her solemn great-uncle Giuseppe who had met her at the train station with a photograph of her in his hand, kissed her on both cheeks, and taken her to his place in a taxi speaking only to point out the Naval Ministry where he had been a government employee. Later she met his wife Clelia and their son Tino, another civil servant, who lived in his parents' apartment, with his wife Anna and two children.

Civil service had been a step up in life for Giuseppe Molletone who had managed to get a minimum education and had gone to Rome as a young man while his brother, instead, emigrated to America. Both of them were poor. If government work was bleak, no work was worse; at the end of forty-five years of tedium, *zio* Giuseppe had his pension while Fran's grandfather, who had only held janitorial jobs, had lived to see his son become a successful businessman.

Fran soon learned of Tino's fascination and envy with his unknown cousin Frank Molletone, and his barely disguised resentment at her coming out of the blissful American blue like a Lady Bountiful with gift cartons of cigarettes, candy for the children, stockings for the women. Tino, who went to work by bicycle to save the tram fare and shaved every other day to conserve razor blades (which he bought one at a time from a street vendor's pack), worked among the archives of documents belonging to the unsettled business of Italy's lost African colonies, and even the liquidation of holdings of deposed Bourbon rulers which went back centuries—a futile, monotonous overseeing of past defeats.

After a week with the Rome Molletones, unable yet to speak or understand quickly, but dreading the big dinners and suspecting that they were spending more than they could afford to give her more food than she wanted, hating the damp chill of the place, the monotony and discomfort, Fran had answered the ad in the Daily American for the room in the Duchess' apartment.

Yet it was a good thing to go to her relatives on that last night of Carnevale; it would quiet some of Tino's suspicions and his sense of injury that though they came from the same origins and had the same name, she, by the twist of fate of the ne'er-do-well brother going to America and becoming her grandfather, was well-off, educated, able to travel and do as she pleased; while Tino, born to the more diligent brother, was cornered in a pitiless life because his father had chosen to remain in Italy. Fran recognized the irony of their positions—she was running from what Tino longed for. But how could he believe that?

Fran stuffed a few packs of Lucky Strikes into her coat pocket for Tino and put some nylon stockings into a bag for Anna. At the corner *drogheria* she bought a box of chocolates for the children and a bottle of *spumante* for the old people. She caught the tram that would take her to Trastevere. The Molletones lived across the Tiber, not in the lively and colorful section which sprawled below the Janiculum hill, but to the east of St. Peter's in an area called Prati that had been fields outside the city until it was reclaimed in the early years of the Fascist regime and made into a depressing urban zone of lower middle-class apartments and treeless piazzas undistinguished by a single monument or any architecture of note. Prati's streets were wide, empty, monotonous, with none of the color and continuous movement of the streets of the city's center.

Fran got off the tram a short block from her great-uncle's apartment. She passed the corner bar where Tino, every week, spent one hundred lire to play *totocalcio*, a betting game based on soccer matches, in the hope of winning millions and changing his life. Arranged around a great circle of dirt euphemistically called Piazza Prati, were several dilapidated apartment buildings.

Fran entered the third one and went up three flights of stairs built with the cheap, grayish stone flooring always present in low-cost housing as a token of grandness. The landings were bare, the doors identical until she came to the one with the brass plate that said Molletone. She rang the bell and Tino came to the door with Anna and old *zia* Clelia behind him.

Tino spoke with a lisp. "*Ciao, Francesca,*" he said, "we haven't seen you for awhile." His tone was chiding. He was short, dark-haired, not carefully shaved and with a certain rakish look about him that could, at times, seem sinister. Fran could imagine him as part of the fascist Black Shirts.

Before her arrival in Rome she had been no part of their lives, nothing to them except a vague entity known as Frank Molletone's daughter. But now that she occupied their city, Tino took it as an affront when time went by without her seeing them.

"*Ciao*, Tino. I've been busy studying and writing for my newspaper at home."

Zia Clelia busied herself around Fran, kissing her on both cheeks and taking her coat while Anna stood by shyly with little Angelo clinging to her skirt. She held in her arms the frail, wizened six-year old Peppino, paralytic from birth.

Fran felt the familiar chill and clamminess envelope her as soon as she stepped into the apartment. There in the corner was the wood-burning stove, seldom lit; down the hall was the acrid smelling bathroom with the broken wooden toilet seat and the faucets that gave only cold water; to the left was the tiny room crammed with a credenza and table which served as sitting and dining room.

"Come, Francesca, come and sit down," the old lady urged, taking Fran's arm and guiding her to a seat at the table. *Zia* Clelia had a pleasant crone face, her smile punctured by empty spaces where she had lost front teeth; her wispy, untidy white hair made a vaporous aura around her head. She was a shapeless faggot bundled into layers of wool and she leaned on a cane, dragging painfully a leg swollen with rheumatism. Her voice was raucous and she had a zestful manner as her voice crackled with laughter. She hadn't left the drab apartment in years, but was more lively than Tino who daily traversed Rome going to work and back without seeming to see or hear anything of interest.

Zio Giuseppe, a dignified and taciturn man, was not yet there. Since retirement he spent his days identically: early mass, picking up the bread and milk for breakfast, and then going out later to shop for the noonday meal, and in the afternoon, playing cards with his old friends until evening. He was seldom at home and, old as he was, he went hatless and coatless whatever the season.

Seated at the table, Fran gave out the gifts.

"Ah, Francesca, you shouldn't disturb yourself for us—you are too kind," Anna said softly. Tino was silent, taking his cigarettes almost grudgingly—not wanting them from Fran, not able to refuse them.

Fran was reminded, in Anna's gentleness and quiet strength of Mr. di Tomasi. In fact, there was something basic and genuine about all the Molletones of Rome that contrasted favorably in Fran's eyes with the pretentious existence of her American family. Even Tino, whose face was often a grimace, showed spirit and courage with Peppino, a child who would never walk or speak; who would have to be spoon-fed, toileted, and carried as long as he lived. When Tino talked to Peppino about their cousin Francesca and where she came from, far across the sea, Fran could see in the child's eyes the spark of intelligence that meant that through the love he received he had also received some connection to his limited world. He had a beautiful face, thin and sensitive, with large burning black eyes. Talked to, he smiled and made low, growly sounds of contentment in his throat.

Tino and his family seemed to have an acceptance toward life that included those who were unfortunate, degraded, miserable. The saints, in which the country abounded, seemed to have shown them how. It was a grace that Fran found peculiarly Italian.

Fresh from a country where the pursuit of happiness and a big wide smile were national marks, Fran thought how Americans loathed suffering: "But how will you stand all that poverty in Italy, it's so depressing," they said before she left. When they went to Europe, it would only be when "conditions are better".

Fran's thoughts filled her as she sat in the chilly room. "Anna," she said, "will you come visit me some afternoon and bring little Angelo?"

"Oh, I should like to! Perhaps some afternoon Tino or *zio* is home to stay with Peppino."

"But you live so far away now," Tino noted caustically.

"Well, it's not America!"

"Do you hear, Peppino *mio*," *zia* Clelia was crooning to the child cradled in Tino's arms. "Did you hear your cousin Francesca say

America?" As the old lady's words came out in a kind of cackle, the boy's thin legs jerked compulsively and his tongue hung out of his mouth even as his little face lit up in a radiant smile and he showed his understanding.

"Show Francesca where America is," the old lady continued.

The boy raised his beautiful eyes to the wall where a photograph of Fran's grandfather hung. Yes, that meant America. On the opposite wall was a florid picture of Venice in glistening satin, souvenir of Tino and Anna's honeymoon there. *Ricordi di Venezia* it said, and Fran wondered if they ever did remember that time.

"Bravo!" cried *zia* Clelia and Tino bent to kiss his son.

Anna took the boy and went off to the kitchen with zia Clelia. "I don't like giving them so much extra work," Fran told Tino who remained at the table with her. She always wanted to help the women—clean the vegetables, set the table, do the dishes, and they always laughed at her as at a capricious child and sent her back to smoke and sip a liqueur with the cryptic Tino.

"What else do they have to do?" he answered her. "They can't travel and write articles. They might as well work."

Irritated, Fran didn't reply. She offered him a cigarette from her pack so that he wouldn't have to open what Fran had given him. He shook his head and said curtly, "How is your friend?"

Busying herself with lighting a cigarette, drawing on it, and then blowing out the match gave Fran time to think. She knew Tino meant Walter, for Walter had come to see her while she was staying there and she had introduced him as a family acquaintace. Ever since, Tino had been curious. Did he surmise that Fran had gone skiing with Walter this past week-end despite her having deliberately mentioned the English women?

"What friend do you mean?" she asked Tino.

"The *marchigiano* who came to see you when you had just barely arrived here. That long, thin guy. You know what we say—*più marche giri, più marchigiani trovi.*"

Fran wrinkled her brow and looked puzzled. "Now what does that mean?"

"It means no matter where you go in Italy, you find the place full of *marchigiani*—especially Rome. From old times they specialized in being spies and tax collectors for the Popes. Your friend is from Ancona in the Marche region so he's a *marchigiano*. So, how is he?"

"Well, for the moment he's neither a spy nor a tax collector. But as a matter of fact, I haven't seen him lately." Fran inhaled and let out the smoke with deliberate unconcern. Then, to allay completely any idea Tino might have of her meeting Walter, she said, "It's easier for you to see him—you work so near to him. If I leave you some extra cigarettes, can you give them to him?"

Tino's immediate reaction was to frown and look worried. Fran smiled to herself knowing that the mere idea of keeping contraband cigarettes in his desk drawer at the Ministry of Finance in order, then, to smuggle them to Walter in the Ministry of Agriculture and Forestry across the street was totally upsetting to Tino.

"That's not a good idea," he answered, his anxiety making his lisp more marked. "I never take these cigarettes you give me out of this flat. If I were seen smoking Lucky Strikes, they'd wonder how I had enough money to pay for them. And if I get caught taking them into another Ministry, that'd be a fine mess. Everyone suspects government workers of dealing in the black market as it is."

"And do you?" she asked, liking to tease him. "Do you deal in the Black Market?"

He made an impatient sound. "Would I be living like this? In any case, as long as you don't see the *marchigiano* any longer, it doesn't matter if you send him cigarettes or not."

Fran smiled with sweet concurrance and said, "I suppose you're right."

It was almost nine o'clock before the old man came in, bringing the *panettone* that was to be served when the couple from the second floor joined them after dinner to spend the end of Carnevale with them. The *panettone* caused a great sensation for it weighed a kilo and cost one thousand lire.

"We should control the weight," declared Tino who never flinched from discovering and exposing small frauds, but had willing ignored the great one of Fascism. Anna weighed the triumphal dome on a kitchen scale.

"One kilo with the paper on," Tino announced caustically, relishing his astuteness. "In other times we paid for the *panettone*, not the paper."

"In other times we had more to worry about than a gram of paper," zio Giuseppe retorted dryly. A man of few words, he had disapproved of the ostentation and references to Roman empire and appeals to *italianità* of the Duce's regime.

The guests were a sergeant of the *carabinieri*, his wife, a boy of about seven who wore bobby pins in his hair, and a girl a year or two older with a big bow perched on her head. The sergeant wore a smoking jacket with a rayon foulard knotted at his throat; he had a beagle face and his hair was slicked down with something oily. His wife was a sallow-skinned, skinny woman who was given to nervous gestures and tittering.

As they all sat around the table, the scene began to have a familiar look to Fran, as if she had seen it in a de Fillippo movie or read it in Pirandello's stories of provincial life. That they were in the Eternal City on its most festive night, seated around a table and calling each other not by name but *sergente, signora, ragioniere, signorina* while Fran waited for their breath to form in front of them from the cold, struck her as something she must have seen in a film.

The two children were called on to recite and they spoke some jibberish that completely escaped Fran but was much applauded at the end. The sergeant's wife seemed to run on a mechanism—she gave jerks of her head and shoulders to communicate attention and when she spoke her arms turned rigid and writhed in circles as each word was forced explosively from her mouth.

For awhile the conversation had to do with the hosts' implorations that their guests eat the *panettone*, the guests' automatic refusals, more implorations, and finally, gracious capitulation. Anna rushed about putting down plates, changing them for each new cookie or sweet that appeared. The *spumante* that Fran brought was opened with great ceremony and the loud bang caused a spasmodic exclamation from the sergeant's wife. They drank, they ate, they spoke in the conventional phrases of people who don't know each other and are wary of dropping conversational clues as to who they really are and what they think.

The evening passed. The Molletones and their guests from the second floor, separated by only one stairway, would go six or seven months or more before meeting again—and then only by chance. Passing on the stairs, they would bow to each other and say, *Buon giorno, sergente... Buon giorno, ragioniere.* The following year, on the night of Fat Tuesday, it would be the sergeant's turn to invite the Molletones to his place. And in a different apartment that was all the same, they would sit at a similar table and feel the same chill while exchanging the same words.

Fran wondered at this closed frugal little world; she wondered at life. She thought of dapper little men like the sergeant or Tino who liked to dance and wear smoking jackets and who, contrary to desire, married skinny, tired women and corked up their lives in drab apartments. Life was hard and yet there was a touching gallantry to how they addressed it with the smoking jacket and panettone.

"*Dottor Bongalli, per favore*," Fran said to the guard at the Ministry entrance. *Dottore, caro dottore.* Walter, too, had his title. And she, only *signorina*.

Names and what preceded them had always been part of her anxiety, she acknowledged. Naming was part of her literalness; if she got the name right, or had the right name, she could then get the meaning right, nail down reality, be sure of things—and that kind of assurance meant confidence.

Subtly, Italy had softened that anxiety. She no longer felt the need to be precise, certain, in command of facts, called on to interpret exactly. Life need not be predictable, orderly, symmetrical; words need not mean all they said, nor titles promise something exact. She was open to chance—let the unforeseen happen! It was what Walter called *l'imprevidibile* in life.

Fran hurried, taking the wide marble steps two at a time and walking rapidly down corridors past dozens of anonymous offices. She was breathing hard, exhilarated and flushed, when she came to his office in the Forestry wing and knocked at the door.

"*Avanti!*" It was his voice, low and firm, strong; with the door still closed between them, and only his voice there, Fran felt his presence.

Walter looked up from his work, fixed her with a broad smile that carried as always a tinge of mockery as did his words: "Oh, it's you. Back from skiing?"

No longer literal, she did not believe the casualness in his words or tone.

"Obviously I'm back," she said with her small smile. As he sat back in his chair and studied her as if measuring the distance, actual and imaginary, that separated them, she added, "And no broken bones."

"No misfortunes of any kind, I hope," he said, taking a cigarette from a pack on his desk and slowly lighting it.

She understood him. And to his probing words, hers made a bridge of assurance: "No, no misfortunes," she said calmly. "I have my notes for an article. The trip was worthwhile."

Walter got up and came to where she was still standing near the door. He put his hands on her shoulders and she felt, as always at his nearness, a tremor of pleasure. But now there was more. The physical edge of longing—what she had learned in the mountains - now tied her tighter to Walter.

"Everything is worth it that keeps you here," he said deliberately, "as long as you don't break yourself in the process."

That was as close as he would get to putting in words that he wanted her there. Slight as it was, for the first time he seemed to make some claim on her, and she liked it. She liked it when he leaned down and brushed his lips over her cheek, saying, "Do you still remember the week of our lives that you owe me? For having waited so long I have accumulated interest and it now comes to more than a week. It's time you paid your debt."

"How?"

Walter took her arm and led her to the chair next to his desk. "These are one of yours," he said as he offered her a cigarette and lit it for her. Leaning back again in his chair, he regarded her placidly and said, "I am glad you came today. I have something to tell you. You will like it, you American girl, because it is like a business deal—you know, like having to go skiing with that professor so that you could write an article."

"Is your deal to go skiing? I would like that," she said, watching his expression carefully. She felt stretched to catch any nuance of his voice, any gesture, any flicker of change in his features.

"Since the last time I saw you," he was saying, "someone in this blessed Ministry remembered that they sent me to America for advance studies and now they've decided they should get something out of it. They want me to go to Florence to make reports to the Forestry school there. But it has to be a long stay because there is also a reforestation problem to look into—a lot of forest in Tuscany was damaged during the war." He paused, watching for her reaction.

"But I don't see what the deal is?"

"What don't you see? If you could see an article in the Abruzzi, can't you see one in Tuscany near partisan hideouts and the battlefields of the Gothic line? Wasn't it your wish to get out of Rome and see something more of Italy... or even of me?"

Fran looked at him in amazement. "You mean I could go with you?"

"Would you?"

"But Lucia..."

"She won't come. She has no friends in Florence and what would she do there alone all day while I was at the school or away doing fieldwork? I don't have to ask myself what you'd be doing— you'd have a dozen articles to do, or you could sketch all of Florence. You could even come with me to reforest the Appenines."

"Oh, yes!" she exclaimed happily, feeling that there was nothing more she could want. But it was too good to believe. "Are you sure about Lucia, has she really said she's not going?"

"In a general way. She's used to my being gone. While I was in America she stayed with her family in Ancona. She has her friends there, her shops, her dressmaker. Right now I am more sure of her not coming with me than I am of your coming."

"Don't say that! I am just trying to understand. When are you going?"

"I leave next week and I'll be gone until June."

"Three months!" Fran gasped. She had never dared hope beyond a fugitive week-end or two. A wildness throbbed in her pulse. She wanted to throw her arms about him and put her head close to his. But something held her back, made her sit there and say, "You must find out for sure about Lucia." She was thinking, how could his wife let him go off for three months? Lucia had met her, had seen her play bridge with Walter—wouldn't she suspect something? Could she be so indifferent to Walter? His being in Florence was not like his leaving Italy for America—she could visit him at any time. And why wouldn't she?

He nodded, thinking, how cool she is, cool as her eyes. Green eyes. Green ice. She is green, too, green all over and ice all over. He would melt that ice into a green pool and plunge with her into that pool. Warm, melted green ice.

"Listen, girl," he leaned towards her, "I will be with Goethe at the usual time on Saturday, and I will know then all that we have to know. Meet me there and I'll tell you for sure to get ready for Florence... and me."

He was so sure, that she began to feel it, too, even though some part of her could not believe in such good fortune. If it were true, she would pack up and leave Rome. She would have three months. She wouldn't think about what came after that. Once the idea of having a limited portion of love had repulsed her. She had neither wanted nor dared to accept so little. Now she was content to have her portion whatever it was. Ironically she thought of the so-called family genealogy which her father had once ordered and which featured a bizarre family stem showing a loaf of bread being divided by two outstretched arms with the interpretation: 'one who is satisfied with a small portion'.

Smiling, happy, she accepted her portion. "Yes," she told Walter, getting up and taking his hands in hers, "I'll come see you and Goethe on Saturday. I passed him the other day and he was looking rather lonely."

"We should have him with us in Florence—he's heard so much between us already, I think he will mind missing the final act."

The final act. Walter had so easily pronounced the words. And she did not wince. Their coming together would be the beginning of the end—what else could it be? What else could he ever give her than a conclusion? For a brief time they would come together and throw into irregular jags the usual pattern of their separate lives. Then the jags would go, the pattern resume. As in the poem called "Portovenere" the professor had read to her.

But when they met on Saturday and sat at Goethe's feet, Fran learned that Lucia had decided to go to Florence, after all. Fran sat quietly as Walter told her; inside her, a dull weight of emptiness had settled, her gaze was clouded. Walter put his arm around her shoulder. "Don't worry, girl, there's always the next time. There has been so far, why shouldn't it work again?"

"You'll be gone until June," she said dully, her voice low and toneless. "What shall I do here? I don't want to be here alone."

Walter shook his head helplessly. "Maybe you could cross the Alps back to Switzerland for another visit." He was sorry for her and he was sorry for himself. Since there was nothing he could do, he tried to help her by assuming an air of nonchalance that he did not feel, for he wanted her to be strong, sure of herself, so sure she could get angry with him. The best way to do this, he knew, was to take lightly what she took seriously. So, affecting casualness, he lit a cigarette and said, "Never mind, you can continue your studies with the professor this way. You did come here to study Italian, didn't you?"

"Oh, stop it! Leave me alone," she cried out. "You know why I'm here! And now what?" Walter had aroused not only anger but also anguish in Fran for his words had brought to mind Balestrini. She deliberately hadn't returned to his classes when she thought she was leaving Rome with Walter.

Walter was taken aback. She had always so successfully masked her feelings with him that he was startled now to see her reveal herself. What he had always admired in her was the capacity for being cool, resistant, teasing, even remote. She had always seemed, sphinx-like, to be laughing at him, herself, their situation together. And it had been this mystery in her that had been the stimulant, the attraction he wanted to get at. Now, she was no different from anyone else in her disappointment.

Fran recovered herself, shrugged indifferently, and faced Walter with a vague smile. "Maybe you're right—I may end up an Italian teacher in spite of myself."

Fran had instructed Amelia to say she was ill when the professor telephoned to inquire about her. Since Walter left, she had resisted his classes in the dark palazzo. Two letters arrived from back home on the same day. One was from the editor of the paper to whom she sent her articles, saying that he liked them and wanted to receive them on a more regular basis. The other was from her parents saying that they would celebrate their silver wedding anniversary with a trip to Europe in the course of which they would meet up with Fran in Rome so they could all return home together. They enclosed a clipping from another paper which was an article written by Sinclair Lewis in Rome.

Their suggesting she'd return with them didn't mean she would. Her own newspaper articles could be her reprieve if she wanted to stay. They paid little, but just the fact of her name in a newspaper by-line would be enough to convince her father to finance her a while longer. But did she want to stay?

The two letters, each in its own way, roused Fran from the apathy she had sunk into and gradually the need for planning and action took over. She decided she still wanted to be in Rome when Walter got back. To secure this, she'd continue the articles and get Balestrini to help her renew her visa.

Walking into the cold, dark classroom Fran saw the professor raise his glance from the papers spread before him and smile at her entrance. "Welcome back, *signorina*, we were sorry to hear you were not well. If you'll stay after the lesson is over, I can give you the material you missed."

She nodded. She was ambivalent about being there and distracted during the lesson.

After the others left, Balestrini asked her, "Were you really ill all this time?—you certainly were well at Gran Sasso."

"Yes," she said. "I think I had flu."

"I've been waiting for you. Let's go over to the Caffè Berardo for something."

Montecitorio was still brilliantly lit as they passed it, crossing Piazza Colonna where groups of young people carried banners with the Picasso peace dove and chanted "Down with war". Communists, muttered Balestrini under his breath as they crossed over to the caffè in the Gallery.

"Do you think that everyone who doesn't want war is a Communist," Fran asked.

His lips curled in disgust, Balestrini said, "The communists are about to cause a riot to show much they favor peace."

From their table in the Gallery, they could see the people gathering in front of Montecitorio.

"But what are they demonstrating about?"

"You see that building all lit up over there," said Balestrini, pointing to the Montecitorio palace. "What passes for the Italian Senate has been in there for days and nights debating the Atlantic Pact while the Communist Party is out here agitating against it. The whole spectacle is as disgusting as only Italian politics can make it. I don't know which is worse—the senators inside squabbling amongst themselves, or the communist punks out here. Shall we leave and go someplace else?"

"No, I want to see what happens. It's news I can write about."

"Ah!—you're thinking of your articles!"

"Of course. I have had a letter from the editor asking for more pieces. It's my best means of extending my stay here."

"Yes, yes, yes! I had quite forgotten. By all means then, let's stay and watch the rioting," Balestrini laughed, caught up in the spirit of the moment.

"Especially since it seems that Sinclair Lewis has been writing that there are no riots in Italy, and now I've got a chance to show how out of touch he is. He's here in Rome, holed up in the Ambassador Hotel and writing what he calls artless letters back home for the Hearst papers. I saw one of his pieces—it's not an Italy I'd recognize!"

"What does he say of us, everything bad?"

"No, that's the trouble, everything is so good! He's in a de luxe hotel suite writing that there's plenty of everything over here—heat, food, courtesy, political equilibrium, Scotch whiskey, and kleenex. He's never ridden with the crowds in the *circolare*, never been in a heatless flat or noticed that families get along with rationed electric power and water available only at certain hours, never experienced the lack of facilities for handicapped children. He's never walked in the back streets to try out Italian courtesy, he lets his dollars buy him courtesy on the Via Veneto. That's all he's seen of Rome so far -that and the movie colony."

Balestrini laughed and signaled a waiter. Fran went on heatedly, "He seems not to have noticed the street-cleaners' strike, let alone the political demonstrations. *His* Italy is the personable prodigal son returned to the fold and fattening up nicely on Marshall Plan funds. It's all the cliché stuff that the people back home love. Americans just love things to go nicely—they can't stand the truth when it involves people being poor and hungry and desperate and voting Communist because the Christian Democrats aren't helping."

"Yes, I suppose it's something like that," Balestrini mused over the drinks which the waiter had brought them. "I saw something in an American magazine about our Sicilian bandit Giuliano. To you Americans he's a Robin Hood -a kind of handsome cowboy type, or a good-hearted outlaw. The public doesn't want to believe he's just a Mafia-connected killer."

"Being an American—a real one, I mean—is harder than just being born there. You have to believe something, too, and I'm not sure just yet what it is."

Balestrini laughed. "So you come to Italy to find out if you are an American or not."

"Not really. It happened while I was here."

"Good! Maybe Italy and I will combine to make a positive person out of you, after all."

The crowds had grown in front of Montecitorio and armed police were arriving in jeeps as the shouting and confusion got louder. Some groups of students in the Gallery started heckling and jeering and suddenly the armed police broke in among them making them bolt like startled deer. A few ran towards the caffè, hiding behind the potted plants which shielded the tables from the Gallery. From behind the shrubbery a few of them continued the heckling.

"See that," said Balestrini disgustedly, "typical Italian bravado. These same guys who are hiding here like rabbits will go home and tell everyone how they battled police guns. Enough of this!—let's get out of here."

In Piazza San Silvestro crowds of people were waiting for buses that had been delayed by the demonstrations. An offshoot of the demonstrators in front of Montecitorio had flowed into San Silvestro near the central post office and were shouting, "Peace, peace! No to war and the Atlantic Pact!" When an empty bus finally entered the square and drew up to its stop, the demonstrators assaulted it, rocking the bus and its terrified driver from side to side in time with their chant. The crowd waiting at the bus stop began to jostle with those blocking them from getting on the bus and as a general melee ensued, the whining sirens of the riot squads were heard bearing down on the square.

"Come on," said Balestrini tersely, grabbing Fran's arm and starting to run towards a doorway. "Let's get in here, the *celere* is coming!"

The riot police screeched their jeeps to a stop in the square even as the sirens kept up their eerie whine and searchlights picked out the rioters who were fleeing. One, hit by a jeep or clubbed, had fallen to the street and several persons stopped to lift him up and take him away. Other of the rioters tried to hide in bus queues or in alley-ways or on church steps, but the celebrated rapid squad smashed over curbs, swerved around corners, hurled up steps, pursuing the fleeing youth or pinning them against walls with relentless determination. The riot was dispersed from Piazza San Silvestro as thoroughly as chaff from wheat in a high wind. Within minutes calm had returned. The bus was boarded and there were no more chants of "Peace! Peace!" to disturb the night.

Fran and Balestrini came out of their doorway. "Sinclair Lewis should get out of the Ambassador bar and see what he doesn't know," she told him.

"And we, instead, should get into a bar. I think we can have a drink before another bus comes."

They stood at the counter of a small bar around the corner from the post-office and had brandy. Balestrini, speaking softly so as not to be overheard said, as he leaned towards her, "Well, tonight you have seen something and you can tell your readers how hopeless it is for a missionary-minded America to want to impose democracy on us."

"Why hopeless? Demonstrating is a democratic action."

"Sorry, that is not the question. The question is, why should

Americans be missionaries? We are an old people and an old civilization, but politically we are still young. It is no good to set up, artificially, a democracy in a country where we are still subject to a dozen tyrannies—from the Vatican in Rome to the Mafia in Sicily." Balestrini shook his head and said bitterly, with a grimace of disgust contorting his features, "How could I be a Christian-Democrat in such a state of things?—and yet, how can I be communist?"

Fran looked at him and wondered if, at heart, he were perhaps still longing for the law and order of the regime. At least there was some predictability then. No, he could never be a communist, even though that was another form of predictability. But by now she knew him well enough to know there was a part split away from him which seemed to act outside of himself like a kind of devil's advocate, upsetting the settled picture of the conventional professor he was.

It seemed as if this curious man yearned to be what in fact he was—a conservative; a quiet, settled apologist of aestheticism who was unconcerned with other details of living in a world filled with beings who were all too distressingly human and fallible. But the devilish small voice of mischief would not let him be at rest—it insinuated that he should make a show, at least, of being interested in reality, being politicallly daring and in the spirit, at least, of the rebels. For a man like him the easy, acceptable position was to express liberal, anti-clerical sentiments. This caused no Italian any moral compunction. Like Balestrini, such Italians went on being observant by committing their children to the same amoral role. He was, Fran thought, a professor who professed too much and meant too little.

Still, puzzled, she asked him, "Why would you even consider being a communist when you've just finished such a bad time with Fascism?"

"My dear," he whispered, "I don't want anything—except you and love."

"No, really," she demanded.

Balestrini gave a comic sigh. "Don't tell me we are going to talk the whole night of politics! After all, as an Italian I am allowed to be apolitical. If we weren't such an apolitical people we would be living in a communist country today. Do you know that we only avoided it by a bicycle race?"

"No," Fran laughed,"but I guess I'm not surprised. Tell me."

"Last summer there was an attempt to assassinate the communist leader Togliatti as he came out of parliament. For forty-eight hours a general strike tied up the country completely and the Communist Party was ready to put into action the plan for insurrection that, in that circumstance, would surely have succeeded. They had the whole nation in their hands and uprisings were occuring in some towns. During the crisis, while it was uncertain whether Togliatti would live or die, Gino Bartoli won the Tour de France— the great classic of all bicycle racing. Radio programs were interrupted and extras came out to announce this Italian victory. The people who were poised one moment for revolution, forgot Togliatti for Bartoli and so Italy was saved. That is the measure of Italians, my dear!"

"Thank God!" she said. "How sensible of them—how civilized and sane."

"And so I'm back where I started, apolitical not courageous enough to be communist."

"Isn't there anything else you could be?"

"Yes," he laughed. "A poet maybe, and a lover certainly. But politically only confused like the rest of the country. You know the Communist League of Young Women had a reunion recently in Modena and do you know what became the keynote of their conference—that De Gaspari had ruined their dreams of finding a husband and having children because his Christian Democrat party did not give matrimonial loans and child-bearing awards! There you have communists fondly recalling one of the worst mass-appeal swindles ever perpetrated by the Fascists. And who were the communist young women led by?—by a millionaire deputy named Laura Diaz who put away her expensive gowns and lovers for the occasion and made herself out to be someone whose spinsterhood was due to that fiend De Gaspari! This is Italy—this is Pinocchio's *paese di balocchi*. The only one who always knows where's he going and how to get there first class, as usual, is the Pope."

Fran was thinking of Mr. di Tomasi, who despite exile and hardship, did not hate his country of birth. And she had told him she never would. And he seemed to her, in his white American kitchen, a gentle Geppetto, the long-suffering father of Pinocchio. And Fran realized the great dignity and worth of Mr. di Tomasi and felt that he, more than the professor at her side, was the teacher who had given her Italian and a sense of who Italians could be.

"How confusing it all is," said Fran wearily.

"Better to think of ourselves and let the others go to the devil. I was hoping you would ask me to come in when I take you home tonight. It's been a long time since the last time."

Yes, thought Fran. And the confusion she had felt about all human affairs she now felt towards herself and her part with Balestrini. But she was too tired to think—it was easier not to. And so that night they were together again.

"Well, are you fed up yet?" her father greeted Fran in a suite at the Hotel Excelsior.

Jenny Molletone, a mink stole drapped over the back of her chair at the dressing table, fanned herself as she addressed Fran. "Your brothers were smart—they chose new cars over a trip to Europe. They'll have something to show for the money."

Her parents were newly arrived in Rome and it was clear to Fran that they themselves were already fed up. Each time she met them anew after some absence, they always astounded her. And saddened her. She realized that despite material well-being they were frustrated people and, deeply hidden and unarticulated, unhappy ones.

It was not a simple situation: having always tried to disentangle themselves from their Italian origins, they still carried with them the look and name of their ancestry, and the limitations of a menial way of thinking. They had achieved a certain status; they could belong to a country club and their children were college educated. The only thing their money couldn't buy was relief from inborn shame.

On the other hand, their non-Italian American friends accepted them on the very basis that they *were* different and lent themselves to funny stories or jokes about 'Yes, we have no bananas,' and could be prevailed upon to serve up Italian food at parties. Fran sympathized with her parents' continual attempt to get a footing in the morass of trying to guess what others wanted them to be - something that seemed to change with the fashions—and made them victims of chronic unease.

The paradox was that in Rome Fran had discovered that she was both more Italian and more American than they, and could accept being both. She felt as if a firm center were building within her: small at first, like a grain of sand, but then the bumps and collisions of life added accretions and around that nub was the developing pearl.

Frank Molletone smoked a cigar, his manner irritable as he paced the luxurious room filled with their luggage. Jenny Molletone's expensive wardrobe lay over the bed and she went back and forth between it and the closet where she was hanging the clothes. "I don't know if I brought the right things," she fretted. "What are you wearing Fran?—oh, that? Haven't you bought anything new? Why don't you ever look right?"

Her father's tenseness made her mother react nervously. Now his eyes were screwed up in critical appraisal as he looked out the window.

"Look at that," he was saying, and Fran, glancing, saw beggars going from table to table on the sidewalk outside Caffè Doney. "That's no way to live!"

"Look at that," Jenny Molletone echoed, "that's just what Bunny Markee told us it would be like before we left. Look at how dirty they are."

"And so is their money," he growled, looking at the handful of tattered lire which he had taken from his pocket to sort out.

Fran could see that they were prepared to be offended at everything in the land. She wanted to show them the beauties of the city as she had seen them with Balestrini before he left Rome for his wife's summer place in the north. But already she felt shy and distanced from her parents.

In the Excelsior bar, they showed her snapshots of themselves on the ship sitting at the Captain's table, sitting on deck, sitting in the lounge, dressed in funny hats for the farewell dinner. They spoke of what important people they had met: a top man from Coca-Cola, a bank president from Cleveland, and Conrad Hilton. Fran knew that when they got home they would have nothing from all their trip to top meeting Conrad Hilton. Nor would the people back home disagree with them. But that was the way it was—her parents and everybody else would think it was she who missed the boat, not they.

Fran watched uneasily as her father had to ask for ice for his drink of scotch and water. Two cubes were brought on a plate. He laughed sardonically and handed the waiter a tip of two hundred lire for which he received a deep bow and profusions of thanks which made him say, almost affably, "We are Italians." The waiter cocked his head in polite and quizzical interest while Fran looked away. "Born in America," Frank Molletone explained, "but of Italian origin."

Fran understood his real meaning: what he was saying was, See us... see how well dressed and what fine looking people we are. Americans, of course, you can tell immediately. And yet we could have been no more than what you are. Our parents came over poor, but we worked hard in America and made money and now we can sit here and be the *gran signori*, and pass out the tips to you. Now we're Italians with no Italy left in us. And don't think we don't know how you envy us -all of you eat out your liver everyday wishing you were in our shoes. That's the whole point of our coming back— to show you what you missed and how we became better than you.

Fran told her parents about *zio* Giuseppe's family in Rome, her studies, and her plans for future articles. Her mother wanted to hear about shops and shopping and her father said, hearing of little Peppino, "Wouldn't you think they'd have him institutionalized."

They decided they would have to pay the relatives a visit. "The plan," her father told her, "is not to stay in Rome very long, but to do a bit of sightseeing in Italy and to take Tino along as the guide. Then we'll all go back together by way of France."

"I'm not ready to leave yet," Fran said. "I want to get my degree in proficiency in Italian from the University for Foreign Students in Perugia. Maybe we can stop in Perugia on this trip through Italy."

"What's there?" her mother asked suspiciously. "I've heard the best place to shop is Florence."

"Mother," Fran said with a kind of weary exasperation, "*every* place in Italy has *something* there!"

Walter returned to Rome. While her parents did an American Express High Points of Rome tour of the city, Fran went to the Ministery: the same guards at the door, the some interminable corridors, the same marble, but now in June the chill felt good.

"*Avanti*," Walter called out to her knock on his door.

She walked in and they smiled at each other. Except for the acceleration in her heartbeat, it could have been only days since they last met.

He got up from his desk with the lazy suppleness which made him both quick and controlled. His lithe movements seemed one with the mental skirmishing he liked so much. His lean, taut face was tanned from months spent in the field in Tuscany.

He barely grazed her cheek with a kiss, asking "How did you make out these months in Rome?"

He spoke casually, as if from unconcern. But she knew this was the way he would put it: his question was about the professor. He would never want to appear anything but restrained. Never too pressing, that would be too un-Walter-ish. He wanted very much to know about her and she was glad of this. Now she would tell him everything. But she matched his casualness with her own.

"Make out in the American sense?" she countered. "Or do you mean how did I survive without you?"

"Are you playing with words—or with me?"

"Neither. After Gran Sasso I did spend some time with the professor. He helped me a lot—with the language, knowing the city, art and music, even myself. But he's gone now, gone and lost forever."

Walter looked at her closely, a long hard silent look. He was seeing something different about her. She was not so tense, not so full of that cat-like nerve that he had known in her. She was more relaxed now, complacent, confident. "I think your professsor must have helped himself, too...." he began.

Fran's lips parted as if to cut in.

He waved dismissively. "You don't have to tell me," he said brusquely, returning to his desk. "I'm not so wooden that way—I think I know about professors being helpful to female students." He laughed sarcastically and leaned back in his swivel chair. "Effects of the war—inflation in everything, even in lovers! Nowadays anyone can become a lover, even a professor. Anyone but a poor forester! But what the hell could I expect? Isn't that what American girls come here for? Why don't they put love-making with the professor on the curriculum so that you can at least get credit for it, along with the other things. 'All professors to be approved by American Express', or something like that, so you can be sure you're getting your money's worth."

She was relieved at his anger. She approached his desk and leaned over, her voice cool. "Why do you say that? he's no more."

"Funny, that you should have shown yourself so strong-minded with me and so vulnerable with him."

"He didn't let me believe he was free when he wasn't," she said in a low voice, turning from him to look out the window.

"He thought he was helping me, and in his own way he was. It was never a question of love—that was never even part of our vocabulary."

There was silence in the small, drab room, the peeling walls unrelieved by any visual matter, even a chart. Fran heard him light a cigarette and then the sound of his drawing deeply, exhaling. It sounded so distant, as if they were in different rooms.

"Our story is rather funny and strange," he said finally and his voice was calm, detached. "Everytime we are to be together, fate intervenes. Do you remember that snowfall outside Luigi's that I disappeared into when we were last together in the states? I walked away into it, eating the snowflakes on my lips. And they were good and sweet and humid. There were lots and lots of things to be said between us that night and we didn't say one. Maybe it was smart. Maybe everything would have finished then. But the night I remember was wonderful... rather magic. And now we are here in sunshine, in another country and another year, but the same things are still unsaid...."

She turned to him, her eyes soft and filmy, as if there were tears just beyond her gaze, tears she wouldn't show. "Are things different now?" she asked.

"Don't say it. Don't think it. Didn't I explain about my Forestry work—about how long there is to wait before seeing the results of a planting? Well, I am a forester, girl, just waiting and waiting. I am patient; I know that when my planting is ready it will be beautiful...

time doesn't bother us too much. Your eyes and greenness, my cheeks and that hollowness you like, your stinkingness and my stinkingness. How many times did we think to have finished between us—and then there was always the next time."

"Yes. My father and mother thought I'd go back with them, but I'm staying."

"Go back? You know sometimes I feel really uncomfortable in all this business. It's just like having eaten all the cherries and then seeing *you* blamed for the theft while I stand calmly by looking at the scene and saying to myself—with the taste of cherries still in my mouth and in that funny sort of voice one has talking with a mouthful of pits—What the hell is going on here? Why don't I tell you, yes, go back with Pop and Mom and start looking for a husband? It would be the only decent and right thing I'd have done towards you since we met."

Fran laughed and shook her head, "I'm not looking here—or there -for a husband. I'm here for myself."

"It would still not be too difficult to destroy myself in your memory in a kind of spiritual suicide—later, yes, it will be too difficult for both of us. And what then? But I'm afraid I'm not the guy to be noble. I don't have the strength and the good will to make you go away. That is me. Do you still like what I am?"

"You know what I like." A note of regret and sadness had crept into her voice, contrasting with the calm of her face. "I'm going around Italy with them for awhile, then I'll be in Perugia. I'll wait for you there."

Walter got up, flicking his cigarette out the window, and went to where she was, taking her face in his hands. "Chin up, girl, you are not really alone, even if it looks that way. You are with lots of things still, and especially with me."

Fran leaned against him, her eyes closed and her face against his. He kissed her forehead. They stayed that way for a moment. As she opened her eyes, she caught sight of a street clock and wrenched herself away in alarm, "Oh my God, it's late! I'm meeting them at St. Peter's to see the Pope!"

He laughed. "Are you going to gain absolution from the Holy

Father?"

"No, gain ground with my own father. I hope he had a good breakfast this morning—yesterday he called over the head waiter at the Excelsior and asked what happened to the Marshall Plan that he couldn't have chilled orange juice as at home. My mother told me about it. I don't think she's enjoying her second honeymoon."

"Maybe she didn't enjoy her first one either."

"Silly! I'm going—any message for either father?"

"Better be quiet with the Holy Father. Tell the unholy one Italy is thankful for the dollars he's throwing around. The war was a bit of a nuisance, cities bombed and a few people killed and all that and we're not completely ready for him yet, but next year, or the next, we'll have chilled orange juice for him. We have to be nice to Pop-like tourists—we are a poor country and we can't tell them to go to hell. With the Pope, be careful. He's a little more clever than Pop."

Fran rushed, feeling conspicuous in a city where others strolled. Roman women sauntered and swayed, stopped at store windows, but never strode with the long, fast pace Fran had. She saw her bus at the corner and ran for it as a few heads turned to watch—it amused Romans to see a person run for a tram.

From the tram stop for St. Peter's Fran still had three blocks by foot to get to the Bronze Door at the Vatican Palace where her parents were waiting for her. She was heated and breathless from the rush and thought of her father chewing on a cigar and spitting his cigar-spit right at the feet of the Swiss Guard. The taxi-driver on the way over had probably gyped him and he'd be swearing about the bastard to her mother who'd be tearful and wearing something unsuitably showy with a lot of jangle bracelets. Why, thought Fran as she rushed into the square, do we have to see the Pope?

But she knew why. It was as important for her parents to arrange an audience with the Pope as it had been for them to be on the same ship as Conrad Hilton. It was also practical: Jenny Molletone would have the dozens of rosaries she had bought blessed by the Pope during the audience and then who of her relatives or friends at home would dare say anything about a cheap gift?

When Fran arrived her mother said, "Where have you been? Do you know the trouble your father went to to arrange this? And I have to stand here and take all his abuse!"

Frank Molletone looked annoyed but was silent. He threw his cigar stub among Bernini's columns and strode imperiously before them, flashing a written permit to the Swiss Guard and passing the Bronze Door. He was, for all to see, on his way to see the Pope and his women followed in his wake.

Dear Readers, Fran wrote in her head, *this is the way to see the Pope: upstairs in the Vatican palace is a group of twenty or so other pilgrims which one joins for the semi-private audience. Then begins a procession through connecting rooms from one tapestried, exquisite ante-chamber to another. In each chamber the group comes to a halt and waits. In each room there's the splendid slouch of the young guards in orange, the pages in red breeches and black pumps who patronize the pilgrims, and the arrogance of the plumed princes from Rome's black nobility as they give their turn of service. Occasionally there's a flash of fuchsia as a cardinal comes in one door and goes out the other.*

Fran interrupted her mental writing to glance at her father to see how he was putting up with the delay. She wondered if he'd call over a page or plumed prince and ask what the tie-up was. But as he remained imperturbable, she suddenly realized that considering himself important, he respected another man's importance; he would, therefore, not only put up with the Pope's delay, but relate it later at home with great relish. He would have kept count: he would know how many rooms they had to sit in and for how many minutes total; he would know how many figures were woven into the wall tapestries and how many dignataries had passed by. Being aware that her father was aware gave Fran a new interest and she began to study the other members of the group. They were recognizable by language: another American couple, a Spanish woman and her son; a group of six German nuns, others. Across the room from Fran a stern mother stood next to her two seated daughters who were dressed alike in gray with black lace veils. The girls sat with their knees apart while an English army officer stared between their legs. Next to the officer, an open-mouthed private gazed upwards at the ceiling murals.

A woman who led the procession through the chambers directly behind the ushers, wore a lorgnette. She had, at the beginning, minutely inspected the other pilgrims and then unequivocally put herself at their head. Her very presence seemed to reduce what might have been a spiritual occasion to the tensions of a mixed social event. Trailing at the end was a young Franciscan monk who had committed the gaffe of kneeling before a gorgeously dressed chamberlain, whom he had probably mistaken for a high prelate, and having tried to kiss his hand; for this he had been smitten by a look of disdain from the lorgnetted woman.

Finally there is a sudden opening of doors and a woman in a long black mantilla who looks of some importance is quickly ushered through the room with a convoy of pages. Two guards in a corner click heels and strike their swords. A quiver of restlessness goes through the group for this appearance makes the Holy Father seem much nearer. And, in fact, pages now go among the pilgrims checking each card against an official list.

Another interval and then something white sweeps into the room. Some of the group rise to their feet, some fall to their knees. The white apparition seems to disappear. Is it the Pope? Will he re-appear?

Finally annoyed, Frank Molletone muttered, "You'd think there'd be some procedure to this thing."

And then the Pope, garbed in white, was among them, a wide moire sash about his middle, a cross of diamonds and sapphires on his chest, a skullcap on his head. He went briskly down the line of pilgrims, which had opened into a horseshoe, starting at the far end from the Molletones. He chatted briefly with each, changing languages with great ease and fluency.

Fran marked the quiet, regular procedure: as the Pope stopped before each person, that person kneeled and kissed the pontiff's ring. Kneel, kiss ring, rise, lower eyes, make a quiet response to the Pope's remark. The Holy Father had rounded the horseshoe and was approaching her father. As Fran watched, her father took the pontiff's patrician hand bearing the sapphire ring of St. Peter and shook it as cordially as if he were at a Rotary Club meeting. The Pope smiled and said, "You are American?"

"We are Italian," said Frank Molletone as he would to any waiter, hotel porter, barber, cabman, or newspaper vendor in Italy.

"I see," said the Pope.

But Fran wondered.

"We come from America," her father continued. "But we're Italian. My daughter is here studying."

"I see. Very good."

The Pope stepped in front of Jenny Molletone. Distracted from the ritual by her husband's non-conformance, she also took the Pope's hand and then made a kind of half-recollected curtsey. The Holy Father smiled. "And where are you from?" he asked.

"America," said Jenny.

At her side Frank nudged her impatiently and said, "he knows *that*! He means where in America!"

"Oh," she stammered, "New York." Fran winced. They had gotten it all wrong.

But now the Pope was standing before her and she felt herself unable to do more than shake his delicate fingers and look into his eyes. He smiled and said, "Are you a good girl?"

Jenny Molletone was heard to say in an undertone, "She'd better be!" Fran, looking intently at the Pope said, "Yes, I try."

"Good," the Pope answered, "very good." He finished the audience and went to the center of the room where he knelt and raised his arms above him in prayer. The pilgrims went down on their knees with Fran among them. Then the spare white figure of the Holy Father, clustered about with his brightly garbed attendants, swept out of the room. The audience was concluded.

Fran left feeling strangely pleased. If she hadn't been absolved, she had at least been recognized. The Pope, a stranger, had looked at her and asked if she were good. Her parents, not knowing in what her goodness consisted, had never asked.

As they went out of the Vatican and into the square, Fran smiled at what Walter had told her earlier. The Holy Father was, indeed, more clever than her own.

Crossing The Alps

From the meltingly soft pink hilltown of Assisi, Fran wrote to Walter: I think it's strange that I end up in the land of St. Francis, my patron saint. When I was a Convent School student we performed a play called "The Wolf of Gubbio" about the wild beast that St. Francis tamed by talking to it. I never believed it. And one of the first things I wrote when I was studying Italian with Mr. di Tomasi was a rhyme about not believing: *Nel lupo di Gubbio/ Io ho gran dubbio.* But now I think I've changed my mind -at least about the *marchigiano* wolf at the door. He's welcome.

Only once on the trip had the Molletones all been moved by the same experience, and that was an encounter with Satan.

In Assisi's *trecento* basilica of Santa Chiara, a striated pink and white stone structure at the edge of town with a vista of all Umbria before it, they had visited the crypt where the body of the gentle, golden-haired Clare is venerated. In that place of almost too-cloying piety and sweetness, there broke through the quiet a scream of such wild and frenzied desperation that it froze them still. The sacristan guide crossed himself hurriedly and Fran and the others watched as a wild-eyed girl was brought, dragged almost, before the tomb of the saint. The girl, no more than fifteen or sixteen, was hysterical and violent; she spit and swore at the young men on each side of her who held her arms and tried to restrain her writhing body.

"Oh my God," said Jenny Molletone, "what's going on here?"

"Don't worry, *signora*," the sacristan told her. "That girl is possessed by the devil. She is brought here so that the nearness of Santa Chiara will help exorcise the evil in her."

Tino crossed himself. Fran saw her father, more awed by the devil than by the Pope, follow suit.

A monk came and stood before the girl, intoning prayers with the impassivity of one reciting his office in a becalmed cloister garden. The girl writhed and wailed and jeered as he chanted the rite of exorcism. When she became suddenly still, the men relaxed their hold on her and then the girl sprang forward and spat on the darkened face of the seven-centuries old saint in her coffin.

Jenny gasped. Fran stared, enthralled. The scene was like some of the early triptychs they had been seeing in museums and churches,

129

where devils, winged, horned, and cloven-footed, were pictured leaving or entering the mouths of the possessed.

Fran felt a surge of compassion for the demonized girl who had been dragged to the depths of the church. It seemed to her that all of them, just by being present at a ceremony which recognized him in that place and at that moment, were possessed by the devil. Evil existed, too, in the mystic land which had produced St. Francis and his thornless roses. Fran wished the girl could be well and free, beyond the power of the intoning monk, beyond the power of either saint or devil. She wished the same for herself: to be beyond powers which could exorcise from her what was thought to be bad and require of her what was thought to be good. She wished freedom for herself. And in the company of her parents and Tino she wondered what made her as she was, and where she was bound. Nothing was clear except who she was not.

In Florence, Tino and Fran separated from her parents to visit Anna's family in the Tuscan countryside. Fran welcomed the chance to get away while her mother and father shopped Florence and they, safely ensconced in another Excelsior hotel, really had no need of Tino and were glad for a day or two to be rid of his dark looks of disapproval as they lorded their way through Italy.

Tino told Fran they would go as far as Vicchio by bus and from there hire a driver to get them to his in-laws in Gattaia deeper in the mountains.

"*Ecco!* that's where the *padroni* live," he pointed out to her from the bus when, every now and then, they passed a cypress-lined drive leading to a magnificent villa visible on the crest of a hill. "And all these people," he raised his chin to indicate the passengers, country people who had come to town for the day, "and Anna's people work to keep the rich in their villas. You will see in Gattaia—all the families there work every minute of their lives for two people, the *Marchese* and his wife. He doesn't work -not even at giving his wife some children!"

"He owns all the land in Gattaia?"

"The land, the farm animals, the machinery, the lives of the people. He lets them work his land and each family gives back half of everything they produce plus any debts they might have run up. Another part goes for taxes, and what's left has to be enough for the families to get through the long winter and start the process all over again. That's life in Italy when you don't live in a villa."

The people she saw actually looked content and vigorous. It was a constant wonder to her that Italians resisted being humiliated and crushed by privation while others, like those who went to America and were cushioned by money, seemed never happy or satisfied. Somewhere she had read it takes three generations to make a gentleman; she wondered if it were the same to make misfits.

It was twilight when the bus stopped in the main square of Vicchio. Tino pointed to a statue in the middle of the classically spare, neat square and said, "You are interested in art, do you know who that is?"

Fran stared at the hooded figure bearing a palette in one hand and said, "I don't know him."

"That's Giotto, and this is the place he was born."

While Tino went into the lone bar on the square to play his weekly *totocalcio* and to find a driver, Fran stood outside to look at the bronze statue in the middle of nowhere and thought of Giotto starting from here to become who he was; she thought how no distance or difficulty had ever kept grace from reaching a people who were, she told herself, her people too.

The driver who was to take them to Gattaia laughed when he heard from Tino that Fran had come from America, had been to Paris, Switzerland, and Rome, and was now on her way to Gattaia. "Nobody in Italy knows where Gattaia is," he told her, "but we all know where America is."

"Your country is beautiful," she said.

"Yes, but maybe not the life."

The country they drove through was still, the cypresses spectral against the darkening sky. The car bumped over a dirt road until it stopped abruptly, as if it had come smack against the rise of the mountains. They were surrounded by complete darkness. Looking from the window, Fran could see nothing.

"*Ecco, Gattaia!*" said the driver cheerfully, pointing out at nothing. Fran and Tino got out of the car and stood in the dirt road. Above, a sky sparkled with star points and there was a vague outline of wooded mountains pressing close on the remote valley. By the car's headlights they made out a farmhouse nearby with a flicker of light, as if from a low-hanging star, coming from it. The night was the intensest dark she had ever experienced; it reminded her of summer camp when she was a child, afraid to sleep in the cabin surrounded by dark and trees, worried by the silence and wishing for home.

"This is it," said Tino, "this is Anna's house, the first one from the bridge on the road to Vicchio."

Fran could make out no other houses, no bridge, no village. She walked blindly, grasping Tino's arm, climbing an inclined drive of thick cobblestones and coming to a space in front of the edifice where wagon shapes were silhouetted in the night.

"*Weh!*" Tino shouted in the doorway. "Here we are!"

The farmhouse came alive with talking, gesturing people who surrounded them and pulled Fran into the large stone-paved room dominated by a large hearth that made up the entire first floor. She met Anna's father, a straight and grizzled old man in an undershirt who gave her a direct look and a firm, strong handshake. He was short and stocky with a weathered brown skin and beautiful clear blue eyes that pierced and startled Fran with their candour. Anna's mother stood at the wide hearth, her sunken face beaming a toothless smile while she mumbled compliments that were unintelligible. Near the old woman were two young girls, her granddaughters, who had come down the mountain for the occasion to see the American visitor and to help out. They were pretty girls, blond and blue-eyed and grave, and they looked as if they come out of Renaissance paintings. Shyly they looked with open curiosity at Fran, but said not a word.

Anna's two brothers, Mario and Pierino, and Mario's wife and children, lived in the farmhouse with the old people. Standing apart, in a corner of the room, watching with the gentle smile of idiocy, was a young man they called Luca, a stray who had somehow arrived in Gattaia as a boy and had been taken in by the family.

Fran felt strange, foreign, in that big room with its huge open hearth where the women manouvered busily over boiling cauldrons and pans of sausage frying over coals. Mario's wife was rinsing greens over some druid-like slabs of granite that made a rudimentary sink. One of the young girls went to a storechest against the far wall and took from it round forms of bread which she placed on the long table in the center of the room, swooshing away the flies that had settled there. Crude wood chairs with rush-woven seats were grouped around the table. The only other furnishing in the room was a blue sideboard on which appeared some dishes, a clock, some family photos of weddings or first communions, and a cheaply framed page from a magazine showing the seven stages of man's life. Two bicycles leaned in a corner near the stairway and on the wall over the stairs was a holy picture with a lighted candle in front of it.

Fran and Tino were seated at the table while preparations for the meal continued. The women timidly glanced up from their work to look at Fran, but did not speak. Only the old man did so. To address Fran he raised his voice, opened his eyes wider, and lifted his brows as if to give weight to his words. He did not address her by name, but leveled a stained finger at her and blared, "You in America.... You in America, do you live on the land? Do you have work for everyone? Do you eat *minestra*? Do you keep chickens?"

Fran liked the old man, his startling blue eyes and simple, strong ways. Mario, the elder son, who was dark haired and dark eyed and resembled Anna in his leanness, was simple and direct like his father. Pierino was different. He was very good looking in the classical Italian way with thick wavy black hair and luminous eyes. But his smile was too flashing, his hair too slicked, his voice high pitched and affected. He, unlike the others in work clothes, wore a yellow shirt open at the neck and monogrammed with his initials, and a wrist-watch. He fussed about the table shooing flies away and correcting the old man's speech. He offered the guests wine. When Fran, in turn, offered him a Lucky Strike from her pack he took it and said, "Ah, American cigarettes! It's a long time since I've had one—since I was a prisoner of the Americans during the war."

"Some prisoner," shouted Mario good naturedly. "He's the one who loaded the bombs onto the planes that flew over us and gave us their droppings!"

Everyone joined in this laughter at themselves and at the wild unpredictability of life.

"Well, what could I do as a prisoner, refuse?" shrugged Pierino. "But the Americans did have good cigarettes."

"Here, have these," said Fran, giving him her pack. Pierino's face lit up like a child's with pleasure.

"What airs!" scoffed Mario. "After seeing Florence he came back and got la Santoni to start embroidering his shirts in the Florentine manner. Now he has to smoke American cigarettes—here in Gattaia! No wonder everyone here says that he's not of this world."

"No matter," Pierino, stung to rebuttal, retorted rapidly. "Now I am a peasant and I can't say I lack for a piece of bread. But I'm not going to stay here and sweat for that bread and a few chestnuts for the rest of my days! All my life I have wanted to be a little well-dressed and to smoke a cigarette when I felt like it. Soon I'll get out of here, as Anna did, and go to the city for work. Is it wrong to want to get ahead?"

"Not wrong, but foolish," said Tino sullenly. "life in the city is no better—maybe worse. The only ones who can do what they want are the Americans like my cousin. They even defecate money."

Pierino turned to address Fran. "I learned to drive an American truck when I was a prisoner in Sardinia. Maybe your father can get me a job in America as a truck driver."

"I'm afraid it's not so easy to come to America right now, unless you have your family there to call you."

"You are somewhat my family—my sister Anna married Tino who is cousin to your father...."

"That's not close enough," Fran said apologetically.

"Listen Pierino, why don't you marry Francesca?" Tino, a little drunk on the strong red mountain wine, laughed boisterously at his own suggestion. "That should be close enough!"

Pierino did not look at all surprised or flustered by the

suggestion and it occurred to Fran that he may have already thought of it.

As they ate, the low, rumbling sounds of the oxen and hogs berthed in stalls adjoining the large room, mingled with the laughter and talk and Fran felt as if she could feel their breath. She wondered what life would be like in such a place. Is this how her ancestors lived? she wondered. No, worse, far worse—this was Tuscany and they were from the bottom of the boot.

At the table Pierino hovered about her, pressing her continually to eat. He helped her to the sauciest part of the pasta, the tenderest leaves of salad, the choicest bits of chicken.

Tino, observing, said to Fran, "Ah, *il boccon del prete* is for you."

"The priest's mouthful?" she laughed.

"Sure—everything of the best goes to the priest, or to the person you want to impress, am I right, Pierino?"

Tino was jovial, outspoken and quite bold that evening in contrast to the surly guy Fran knew in Rome, so full of hesitations and repressions.

"Right!" shouted Mario. "And you should see what a *boccon del prete* little Carla has become. If Pierino doesn't hurry up and marry her the best parts will all be gone!"

The men laughed raucously as Pierino, indignant and flushed, tried to shout above the laughter. "Mind your business! Who I marry is *my* business!"

The old mother had been at the hearth all this time. Finally she came to the table and sat next to Fran. She didn't speak to her directly, but looking straight ahead said as if to herself, "What nice hands the American has."

There in the glow of the hearth, on that still, cool summer night somewhere in the Appenines in a place called Gattaia, Fran felt cradled in the immensity of the universe. Outside in the courtyard when she got up from the table to look at the night, she saw only the reaches of blackness that were sky, hills, and woods. Here and there the darkness was punctured by a point of light, but whether from stars or farmhouses she could not tell. The silence was complete, not an engine throb, not a call, not a footfall.

And there came to her mind the lines from Eliot's *Four Quartets*, which she had taken as emblematic of her relationship with Walter:

Footfalls echo in the memory
Down the passage which we did not take
Towards the door we never opened....

Never had she been in such quiet, so removed from the world. It made her think of her reason for eluding Walter: the fear of everything ending. And in all that space and dark, like an intimation of eternity made visible, it seemed like no reason at all.

That night she slept in the parents' bed upstairs, between coarsely woven linen sheets embroidered with the old woman's initials. One of the young girls, looking like a Botticelli maiden, had come to fill her wash basin with water and show her how to empty it from the window onto the front court below. She had given Fran an elegantly woven raffia ring and told it went on the seatless toilet off the hall.

Awake, when Fran threw open the shutters to let in the day, Gattaia, or her vision of it, was pulsing with activity. She looked from the window at chicken and ducks and little children swarming over the front court where wagons of corn and grain were drying in the sun. She could see the rest of Gattaia, a little huddle of gray stone houses along a dirt road, which wound its way to the bridge over the stream near the boldly painted dark red farmhouse where she was staying.

Luca looked up at the window and smiled at her. Mario was leading oxen to the fields. A little girl came up from the stream with a pail of water in each hand. Up in the hills Fran could now see other farmhouses, tiers of olive trees, the beautiful coned haystacks of Tuscany, fields and forest. The day was beautiful with sunshine and life and she was filled with a sense of deep sweetness towards the earth and the people.

Tino was at the big table having *caffè-latte*. The old woman was plucking freshly killed chickens, and pasta had already been made and was drying on a rack near the hearth. Children wandered in and out of the farmhouse, barefoot and solemn. Mario's wife and daughters bustled about with brooms and pails of water. The day had begun and each person of the household had a task—each of them, from child to the old toothless woman knew what was expected and how his or her life would run that day. Each of them, except for Pierino accepted what seemed ordained. It was the same everyday; the variables were the seasons and the ritual functions of life—birth, baptism, marriage, death; the rest was unvarying, leavened by the precepts of a collective wisdom which had its origins in that land and in the people who had lived upon it for millenia. Even as Fran admired their certainty and serene steadiness, she did not want to know in her own life that there was but one way.

Later Tino and Pierino took Fran through the village to meet other relatives of Anna's. "Amuse yourselves," the old mother had cried out as they left.

"How do you amuse yourselves here," Fran asked Pierino.

"A few of us sometimes put on plays in the schoolroom. Or we talk or sing or go the Signora's to improve ourselves. Now, in good weather, we dance in the cleared area near the *People's Co-orporative*."

Even for someone like Pierino who wanted more, it did not seem to Fran too poor or mean to be amused that way.

They passed neat fields redolent with fragrant hay, grapevines, corn and olive trees. Life seemed pleasant and easy in Gattaia on a summer day. From the bridge Fran stopped to look at the girls who were laughing and talking as they beat wash over rocks in the stream. Tino was observing her.

"They do it in January, too, when they have to break the ice over the water and their hands become red and swollen with the cold. Not many can go to school in Vicchio after they're ten years old—they're needed to work."

Fran understood. Life was simple, but the terms were hard. She admired the handsome, fresh looking people she saw along the way; hard-worked they may be, but none looked cowed and resigned. They greeted the village priest, a big man in a soiled cassock whose face bore permanent scowl lines even in repose; they met the school-teacher, the miller who was the head of the local communists and had once, in his youth, lived in Philadelphia, and even the pretty girl named Carla who everyone referred to as Pierino's *fidanzata*. And wherever they went in the village, dozens of children ran after them with the alacrity of grasshoppers while silent black-garbed women stood still to stare.

The woman Pierino referred to as the Signora was the village dignitary, a great hulk of a woman in her late fifties who had lived in a three-story walled villa that had been the finest building in Gattaia until it was bombed into nothing but rubble, not even the walls left. Now she lived in the back room of a hovel off an alley across from the ruins. She complained of heart palpitations and leaned heavily on a cane; she had frizzled dyed red hair and wore horn-rimmed glasses over thin penciled brows. She recieved them in the room she occupied, its walls plastered over with advertising posters and the ceiling hung with strings of drying herbs and toma- toes. The sight of her knitting together bits of colored rags as she sat in a squalid room filled with the presence of laughing handsome girls in toothpaste ads struck Fran as some giant hoax of fate. Re- duced so low, she was still imposing, fearful, awesome and Pierino and the others treated her with great respect.

"*Jolie fille*," said the Signora when Fran was presented to her. She insisted they get out of the shack and go sit in the shade of a tree that remained where once her pleasure garden had been. She sat on a wooden bench and contemplated the desolation where her home had been. Nearby was the modest patch of cultivated ground where she now grew the beans and tomatoes of her livelihood. Here, in the good weather, she held court with Pierino, Carla, the school-teacher and a few other young people of Gattaia who sought to improve themselves in conversations with her. During the winter, the shack with the advertisements on the walls was her salon.

"You meet me at an unfortunate moment in my history," the Signora told Fran. "Before the war I had a home—not the nasty room you saw me in—and I had a car. I traveled, like you. I know it is a fine thing to travel, to see oceans and cities and not always the cursed ring of mountains around this village." She shook her cane in rage at the implacable ruins and at the wild beauty of the mountains, which were always in her view. "I'm in a bathtub," she cried, "a monstrous tub that I can't get out of." Her rage was splendid, and not the carping complaint of Frank Molletone missing his morning orange juice.

From the Signora's place, they ascended a rocky path by the far side of the stream to the house where Anna's sister lived with her husband and children, two of them the young girls who had been present in the farmhouse the evening before when Fran and Tino arrived. Seen from on high, Gattaia was idyllic, the fields a wonder. But distance was the touchstone. From the heights, there were no flies swarming over the food, no animal droppings wherever one walked, no grave-faced children working in fields or washing laundry in streams.

Anna's sister, Paola, had the same blue eyes as their father. Her husband was a big, jocular man and they all sat at a table in a neat room with white-washed walls to have biscuits and a sweet wine.

"How do you like Gattaia," Paola asked Fran.

"I think the country is beautiful."

"Oh, yes," said Paola's husband winking at Tino. "For birds of passage. We're at the end of the line here. After us, only mountains and forests. Only the birds can get out."

"The end of the line, maybe, but the Germans got here," said Pierino.

The allusion to the war made Fran think of Walter when he was with the British hammering at the Gothic Line. Maybe he had been in this valley, maybe he had helped level the Signora's villa.

"What misfortune!" said Paola's husband. "For centuries no outsiders ever came to Gattaia and then during the war we got them all."

"You got me, *romano di Roma*, before the war," said Tino grinning affably and referring to the time of his military service when he had met Anna and taken her out of the hills to the city.

"Yes, some foreigners have always managed to creep in," his brother-in-law joked affably.

And now it was Fran who was the foreigner, but she felt not at all foreign there.

Coming back down the mountain towards the farmhouse they met an old bent woman all in black whom Pierino greeted as Vittoria. She became speechless with wonder when Pierino presented Fran who had come from America. Incredibly old and hobbled, Vittoria was too shy to address a stranger so she spoke in furtive, whispered words to Pierino: "What language do they speak for the most part in America?... ah, what a beautiful thing to speak a strange language...tonight I won't sleep for the beauty of this day... I am in love with the pretty girl." As they parted, old Vittoria clutched at Pierino's arm and Fran heard her say, "Thank her for coming, Pierino. Tell her we won't forget her."

Fran thought they were the words she herself should have spoken. It was she who was thankful for having come to Gattaia, she who would never forget the people there.

And she even understood better the fear her parents harbored towards the land of their own parents; the wretched villages of Calabria and Sicily from which they had immigrated. Fran understood their confused feelings at the truth of their past—they were more vulnerable to it than she. She was already two generations away and shielded by material well-being and a good education. It was no small gift.

Tino and Fran left Gattaia the day after they arrived. From Vicchio she sent Walter a postcard of Giotto: I have been to Gattaia and it sounds from its name as if it should be full of cats and your kind of place.

From Venice she sent him a photograph of the touring party in St. Mark's square surrounded by pigeons: her father scowling at the bird on his shoulder, her mother smiling fully into the camera, Tino looking sullen with disapproval, and she herself pouting into the distance.

The last card she sent him was brief: The parents' Trip is over. I'm leaving Rome. I'll wait for you in Perugia.

Part Three

Leaving

The decline of summer was in the air. Days were shorter. There was a different light over things as Fran passed through Umbria on the bus to Perugia. The weather held and the landscape seemed immemorial, taken from some painting in which it was a backdrop with walled towns and trees and peasants. Fran seemed to have seen it all before, or to be recalling images imprinted on her imagination before she set foot in Italy.

She had to become wary of such beauty, of the peace that lay over the hills. She had a presentiment of a future in which none of this had any part, and of the solitude in which basically all lives are spent. From the bus window, Fran could see everything looking suspended, separate, solitary: the pair of yoked oxen, each cone of hay, each row of cypress, each farmhouse seemed detached from time. She felt as if the mysticism of the Umbrian saints must have been as actual in this land as the slow crawl of glaciers had been in the area of her home town when it produced the drumlins where she had once skied.

How could she go back again? And yet it was fixed. After Perugia she knew she would go back. Down another valley, up another hill, they approached the town. Should she have stayed in Rome, simply changing her room so that Balestrini, returning from his summer vacation, would not have located her? Rome was compliant and easy; everything was glossed over there in a fusion of many people, many ages, many beliefs. But just for that she had chosen Umbria. She liked some rigor in her life. She needed to make choices.

By slow ascent, with the bus in low gear, they went through the medieval town gates and up curving avenues, arriving at last in a piazza looking like an elaborate operatic stage set: *duecento* Communal palace on one side, cathedral on another, and between them the stunning Pisano fountain ringed by tiers of steps.

A short white-haired woman came up to Fran as she waited for her luggage. "You are the American? You are staying with signor Gabiani?" When Fran nodded, the woman continued, "I am Annaghita, I will show you the way."

Hoisting the larger of Fran's suitcases to her shoulder the woman crossed the square and started down a street which descended steeply towards the ancient Etruscan Arch visible at its end. The street was narrow and dark, bounded by thick stonewalls and paved with uneven, lumpy cobbles that Fran stumbled on repeatedly. Halfway down Via Rocchi, Annaghita opened a door to what seemed a musty cavern and went up two flights of stairs. The entrance to the apartment where she would be staying filled Fran with a dismaying sense of damp.

The bronze nameplate over the door where Annaghita stopped was incised with showy calligraphy and read, Conte Lorenzo Trono-Gabiani. It was the name Fran had chosen from the list sent her by the University for Foreign Students. Annaghita pushed the bell and almost immediately the door was opened by a big, smiling, blowsy woman in a faded bathrobe pulled in tightly around her waist by its cord. She smiled even more broadly as she saw Fran. Fran stared at the women's false teeth and her first sensation was one of embarrassment.

"Ah, the *signorina!* Welcome to our home. I am Signora Gabiani. Did you have a good trip? Are you tired? Come in, come in. Annaghita, take the suitcase into the bedroom on this floor. Come and see your beautiful room, *signorina*, it's full of sun and light. As soon as you wrote, I had Annaghita clean it from ceiling to floor. You'll like it here—the University is just down the street after you pass through the Etruscan Arch. Very convenient, you see. And what a cook the count is, fantastic!"

The woman was loud and showy and continued to chatter. Fran, feeling out of sorts, was relieved only when she reached her room and saw that it was indeed full of sun and light. She would have liked to unpack, sit down at the desk and write a note to Walter, open the doors to the balcony and look out over the street, or lie on the bed and just think. But the Signora, she saw, was not going to leave her.

"Our best room, *signorina*, just for you." She said this with an expansive opening of her arms as if she were about to deliver an aria. "You'll have a lot of quiet here for studying—the room next to this is vacant because my son isn't here, and I put my other boarder downstairs, near the kitchen, where the count and I also have our room." She hesitated a moment, as if not quite sure of Fran, then winked and said, "You won't mind not having the other boarder in the room next to yours—he's very short and dark, from the south, you know, and only a civil servant. I'll wait to fill the vacant room with a better type."

Laughing coarsely, the Signora sat down on a rush bench and motioned Fran to come sit next to her. "Oh, I've forgotten my cigarettes," she said with a great show of distress, "and I wanted to offer you one."

Fran opened her bag and took out a pack, offering the woman a cigarette.

"Oh, thank you. You shouldn't disturb yourself, but I'll accept for courtesy so that you won't feel bad. You'll like it here, *signorina*. My husband—well, I call him that, he isn't really—is tremendous, a real cultured gentleman. He's been a dancing master, a chef.... I'm sorry my son isn't here, too, but he's doing his army service just now. What a shame—he's about your age, you'd get along fine. But don't worry, I'll see that you're not lonely. Do you have any friends here? Oh, yes, I almost forgot—this telegram came for you."

She dug in her pocket and pulled out the telegram saying cheerfully, "Don't mind me, go ahead and read it."

Fran felt the woman watching her open the telegram. It was from Walter. Welcome to Perugia, and welcome to me, it said in

English. Fran looked up and said, "It's not important, just a friend sending greetings."

"Well, he must be a good friend. Maybe he will come to see you in Perugia and he could stay here in the vacant room—it would be cheaper than a hotel, you know, and nearer to you." The woman laughed raucously and Fran thought that by the end of the afternoon, she would know everything about her.

"Now let me help you unpack, signorina." Before Fran could say no, she had opened a suitcase and was taking things out. "Ah, *bella*," she exclaimed, holding a nightgown up to her, shaping it around her robe, and looking at herself in the mirror that fronted the large wood wardrobe. "We don't have nice nylon things in Italy—and look at all those stockings! Once I had such fine things, all silk, too. But not now."

Despite her being so invasive, Fran could not dislike her. There was in her very greediness and attempted cleverness a kind of naïveté, so open that it was almost refreshing.

The woman made a queer match to the count, whom Fran met that evening in the kitchen at supper. The kitchen was down a flight of dungeon-like steps and there, in a low-ceilinged room hung with the season's first grapes, warm with the heat of the stove and comforting with the smell of cooking, the count passed all his time. He was a stooped, grarled man with a shaggy, unkempt moustache and a quizzical, dour look behind his glasses. He was much older than the Signora and though Fran had no way of knowing whether his title was real or improvised, he was, in his way, aristocratic. He reminded Fran of white Russian nobility who had adapted to teaching dance or re-creating as chefs the grand food that had once been served to them.

The count loved to cook. He regaled them at mealtime, when they all met in the kitchen, with fantastic stories of his youth. He also painted landscapes on pieces of rayon for cushions. Tacked to the wall beside Fran's bed was a backdrop of an eagle with coronet that was his work and that never failed to startle her when she opened her eyes to it in the morning. While the Signora jealously kept the packages of American cigarettes that Fran gave to both of

gnarled

them, the count kept rummaging through his pockets for butts, opening them to salvage what tobacco was left and rolling them again in dirty, flimsy paper wrappers that flamed up when he lit them. He was as indifferent to Fran's cigarettes as he was to the made in the USA lighter, typewriter, and camera which enthralled the Signora and that she kept mentioning to Fran.

Each day she came to Fran's room on some pretext. She would ask Fran if everything was all right, if she would like some grapes to pick on while she studied, if she would like to take a walk. Whenever Fran did go walking with her, the Signora got dressed in her best and took Fran along the Corso to point out things in store windows that she'd like to have. Then they'd end up in the fashionable *caffè* of town, where the Signora would offer Fran an aperitif and then not be able to pay because she had left her money at home.

Beneath her toughness, there was all the sentimentality of an instinctive nature. She too, she told Fran, had had her share of disillusionment. And one night in the kitchen, as the count read from the paper of one more abandoned woman who had shot her lover, she exclaimed, "What are women to do—we go through life expecting the one man who is meant for us. It's like trying find in a barrel of halved apples the one half we're perfectly matched to. So what happens?"

"*Storie!*" replied the count indignantly. "There's no such thing as the perfect match. You might just as well grab as many apples as you can as wait for the perfect half to turn up. What nonsense!"

"Still," said the Signora truculently, "it is love that makes the world go round."

"And know-how that greases the wheels," the count retorted.

With the count it was different. When Fran walked with him it was a cultural outing; not for him the bland, commercial Corso. Despite his age and gout, he led Fran up and down the tortuous streets of the Dog, the Stars, and Gold—streets that were already old and in disrepair in medieval times. He would wear an old fedora and shuffle along with his walking stick, speaking to her only in

145

French and looking with disdain upon the townspeople. His teeth were bad, his clothes seedy, his nails filthy, but he had a distinction that completely eluded the Signora.

Walking with Fran, the Count recalled to her the proud names of Perugia's *condottieri*–the Fortebraccio, the Baglioni, the Stratta. He waved his cane in wrath at the lovely Renaissance loggia atop the Etruscan Arch and said it was a pigsty, a modern travesty on an ancient monument. He led her through a vaulted street called Way of the Poet and out the Gate of the Almond to see an old temple once sacred to Vesta. He went though the history of the Guelphs and Ghibelline factions in Perugia as if they were more immediate to his life than Fascism or Communism ever were.

In the kitchen he was given to ribaldry. At night when they all sat together after the evening meal, he would read the paper aloud interspersing the items having to do with adultery or other sexual mayhem with his own witticisms. His face red and bleary-eyed from excessive wine, his elegance gone, he sat and made his remarks in a dry, detached manner that was accompanied by the vulgar guffaws of the Signora. She, on the other hand, was always pointed whether confiding to Fran that the count no longer gave her pleasure in bed, or speaking of the town whores and specifying each one's speciality.

Fran began classes in the palace, which housed the courses for foreign students. By day she sat in rococco rooms where cherubs adorned the ceilings of some past and defunct noble family. By night she sat in the kitchen with its festoons of drying plants and fruit. She would walk out of town and sit in olive groves to sketch. The time went easily.

She sent a card for Walter to come and signed it Zingara. (What he had said was, Do you know what I shall call you? Zimbola. Or Zagara. Somewhere in my life I seem to have heard the word, but now I don't remember if it's the perfume or the flowers of the orange trees in spring. Yes, that will suit you—with one change. It should be lemon trees, not orange. More astringent suits you better. Zimbola or zagara? Let's breed them and make zingara. Yes, there you are, Zingara, the gypsy girl.)

Fran found the Italian autumn a gentle, golden season without the snap and flamboyant color of the American one. It was a mild fall day when she and Walter walked back to the center from the Perugia train station, some distance below the old walled town. She had gone to meet him, and now they ascended slowly, walking closely, hand in hand.

At Porta Sole they stood at the low wall setting off the square and looked silently over Umbria. There on another hill was Assisi, and in the hollow between the two towns was Santa Maria Novella, and away, beyond the hills and out of sight, the rest of the world.

"Dante put Porta Sole in his Paradiso," said Walter softly, "and now I know why."

She turned to look at him as he gazed into the distance and she saw his eyes narrowed in thought, his face lean and strong and looking serious. He had the look of her Cassius painting. "I'm glad that you've come," she told him.

"I will again.... if you want me. It's easy enough to arrange by fitting it into my return trips to the field station in Tuscany."

"It's funny how things worked out."

"Not funny—it was time."

They walked through town, down Via Ulisse Rocchi, through the Etruscan Arch and past the palace of her lessons to where the tram line ended and the fields and olive groves began. They went down a road and passed groups of workers in the vineyards gathering grapes into baskets for the pressing. "*La vendemmia*," he said, the grape harvest.

As they stopped to watch, one young fellow came close by them with his load and Fran asked, "Will you press them by foot?"

He looked at her mockingly and asked in return, "And don't you think it a beautiful thing to crush grapes with the feet?" She heard the taunt in his answer—it sounded like Walter. It sounded, she realized, like all Italians who, *dottore* or not, were quick-witted and outspoken.

Beyond the vineyards, they climbed a low hill into an olive grove and rested on the ground beneath the gnarled branches of an ancient twisted tree. The day was filled with the scent of grapes ripening in the gentle September sun, of farmers far-off calling to their oxen, of the natural stream of life pulsing through the land. Fran lay with her eyes closed, overcome by the happiness of the moment.

"*Sei stanca?*" Walter asked. The words, "Are you tired?", covered her like a caress. She felt how unbearable it was to be so full of love. She could not always stay in Perugia and turn into a rag of a thing—a thing of parts and incoherence, a pastiche of rationalizing that kept her fragmented and not whole. Walter was whole. He knew who he was and he was all of one piece. He dealt simply with things—even his initial duplicity with her had been, in his way, simple.

He bent over and kissed her. "Do you know how I should like to kiss you," he murmured in her ear. "I would like to make love to you only by kisses—kissing you all over for a long time. A very long time. From your ears, to your neck, to your lips, to your shoulders... slowly... a kind of eating and drinking and kissing all at the same time. All over you... your belly... your breasts, every part of you, for a very long time... my lips and my hands never leaving you."

Her eyes became moist as she opened them and gazed at him.

"The green ice of your eyes is melting, girl, just as I predicted. I've come for my harvest, my *vendemmia*. It's a long time to wait, even for a forester."

Vendemmia, she thought, not vendetta. How lovely was their Italian fall, their Umbria, their being together.

They met that night in love for the first time. He came to her room and lay down beside her and fondled her hair as he spoke very low, barely audible even in that silence. "That son of a gun of Shakespeare should have called it a Mid-Autumn's Night Dream... I think it has been all worthwhile, my girl, all the waiting and the tricks, to have such a night as this. I never thought I could have such a feeling for someone... do you know how I feel?"

She knew. She, too, had never before had such completeness, such awareness of being totally herself without opposite and conflicting feelings. It was like finding home.

"I love you, I do love you, and I don't care about the rest!"

It was the first time Fran had ever spoken the word love to Walter. It was something she had always kept from him, as a matter of pride.

She lay in his arms, her hands caressing him, her face pressed against his. "I love you, forester. I love the way you walk. I love your voice and the way you talk and the way your words make love to me. I love the bones of your face, the hollows of your cheeks, the long fingers of your hands. I love your beard rubbing on me... I love all of you. I love you serious, I love you laughing at things. I love you waiting. I love you for loving me. I love you, and now I've told you."

"I am glad you told me. It is worth hearing after all the hell you led me through. Now show me you love as any other woman would, without resisting, without playing games, without your made-in-America mind taking charge. Show me."

They slept in each other's arms. But he was gone before she woke. From then on he managed to get to Perugia, either as a side-trip to and from Tuscany, or coming up from Rome on the early morning train and going back that evening. She'd meet him at the station and they would go back to her room, spending the few hours of his stay there. Occasionally he could spend a whole day and a night with her. He arrived when he could—at two in the morning, at seven, at noon, or in late afternoon. Often their time was reversed from that outside them; then they seemed alone in a dormant city, alone in special, privileged world that was beyond the routines of normal lives.

The Signora missed nothing. Technically, when Walter came to visit, he was given the empty room next to Fran's, which he paid for even though he spent all his time in Fran's room. The Signora smiled conspiratorially at Fran, glad of the extra revenue, and said nothing. It was she who brought Fran those hastily scrawled letters in the orange Ministry envelopes marked *urgente, espresso* which told Fran on which train Walter would arrive. Fran made a gift to the Signora of the American camera she coveted.

One day they went to Lake Trasimeno. The count made them a cake fragrant with anise and Fran had the remains of a bottle of

Napoleon brandy. Walter had brought great packs of photographs to show her and she saw his life in pictures, from boy to man in the time before she had known him. She showed him the sketches she had done in Perugia; she told him of her fellow students at the university. Most were European but finally an American had arrived on a Fullbright scholarship. She laughed as she recounted the American's asking her, "What is your status here?" He meant, of course, what award or scholarship has directed you to the middle of Umbria? It must have been inconceivable that she could have come on her own, unstipended and unofficial. How could she, Fran continued to Walter, explain to such a bright fellow that she was allowed to come to Italy just for its own sake? how could she tell that to someone who was granted thousands of dollars to have Italy as subject matter?

They walked along the lake and she watched him skip stones on the water, telling her each time how many skips he would get. She thought, how well he knows himself; in all things he knows what he can expect of himself. She never tired of watching him.

It was almost November, the chill in the air and the early morning mists were heightened, when Fran received an *espresso* from Walter that November 1st was a holiday for him and he could arrive in Perugia the evening before and spend the next day with her.

It was late when he came to her room, a light rain had started. Fran took him by hand onto her balcony, which jutted over the street. At the movie-house next door the whiny, tinny music of an American western had ceased. Lights were out in Perugia, and only the candles in her room flickered on in the dark. "It's Halloween in America," she said. "and here it's the vigil of all the dead and departed souls."

"How good the air is this night," he said.

They stood on the balcony listening to the rain until Fran began to tremble with cold. Walter led her back into the room, to her bed. The night of the dead souls and the rain heightened their pleasure with the sense that this, too, would pass.

The morning, late, Fran watched from bed as Walter prepared

to shave in the basin that stood on the commode near the window. She loved to see him his eyes narrowed, his arm curved up to hold his cheek taut, he face lathered, his blade working skillfully about his face.

"I would like to see such a show each morning," she said. "Will you think of me each morning when you shave?"

"Yes, I will think of you each morning. And even more than each morning." He turned from the mirror to look at her. "You've never been sorry, have you, about how we are?"

"No, never! Have you?"

"Do you know me?—I don't think I can ever really be old or too fed up with anything from now on in my life. Not with your words in my head, and the memory of loving you in all my body. But I wanted to be sure how you felt."

"Be sure of me—how silly! Can't you tell how it is with me?" She laughed at him, but something like a chill took her. The room was cold, the day was cold, but it was another chill that now made her tremble under the covers. She would not speak of it. He might tell the truth.

It was the Signora, not Annaghita, who came to the door with a tray of caffè-latte and rolls for them. "Aren't you going out today?" she said, "It's *Il Giorno dei Morti* today, a very big feast in Perugia! You must go see, *signorina*, it's very characteristic."

All Soul's Day in English, but the Day of the Dead in Italian. Fran wondered what feasting they could do for the dead.

Walter answered the Signora. "I think we'll just stay here a bit longer. I have to leave by the early train this evening and we don't have much time left together." He spoke quietly without any special emphasis but there was something in his manner that made Fran attentive and the Signora unwilling to press them any further to the festa outside.

"*Va bene*," she said. "I'll have Annaghita set up a table here for you for dinner. That way you can be alone and have time together while you're eating. And I'll tell my old man it will have to be something special today—no sausages, today, *per bacco!*"

Annaghita had brought a paté from the country, and that was

followed by chicken roasted with black olives and polenta browned in the pan juice. A table had been set in the middle of the floor so that Walter and Fran were reflected in the mirror of the wardrobe, laughing and spirited, as they drank a fine golden wine. Fran felt flushed and glowing from the wine and from happiness. Annaghita came and went with each course until she brought the *caffè espresso*, and then they were alone again.

They made love and as they lay quietly, after, Fran murmured, "The Day of the Dead. It should be a nice time to die, when one is so happy. Like leaving a party at the best moment, so all the memories are good."

Walter was quiet, withdrawn. She tried not to notice, but she did. "I think we should go out, now," he told her. "I would like you to see the festa." He did not say, ironically, as he might have—it's something you can write about for back home. He gathered his few things and put them in his brief case. "I won't come back here. I'll go right to the train when it's time."

Out on the Corso they joined the crowds who had thronged to Perugia for the street fair and celebration, which was to last eight days. All the nougat makers and clothes vendors of Italy seemed to have descended upon the town's main square. In Piazza Porta Sole, an amusement park had been set up with carousel, camels, and performing midgets. The Corso was jammed with rickety wooden stands and throngs of country people who gawked at the sellers of wares crying out to them in all the accents of Italy. Fran, delighted, held on to Walter as the press of the crowd carried them forward. They stopped to watch a pottery seller juggle saucers, they bought fried *bombe*, hot and sugary, and looked for a gift for the Signora.

At one stand Walter stopped her and said, "I see something here I want to get for you." He picked up from the pile of trinkets of all kinds a little chest made of fine polished cedar wood with a reddish cast and a pleasing acrid smell of wood smoke.

"This is what a forester should give you," he said.

"What is it," she laughed, "a hope chest?"

"Not for hopes—for remembrance. But maybe a hope chest isn't such a bad idea. I would like, someday, to know you have a husband

and have joined the nice gray ranks of humanity—it's often the best satisfaction."

She raised her brows in puzzlement. "I shall keep your letters in it. Why are you talking about husbands and joining the gray ranks? I don't want...."

He interrupted her brusquely and said, almost angrily, "It is not always what we want, but what we must do."

"You are very strange today! Do you know what I must do? I must ask the count to find me a turkey—it will soon be Thanksgiving. If you're not able to come on the real Thanksgiving day, the day closest to it when you do come will be our Thanksgiving. Do you know when that will be?"

He took her arm and said, "Let's get away from these people for a little while."

A narrow back street beyond the Duomo led them down to the encircling town wall in a deserted part of the city that overlooked the land beyond. They sat on a bench near the wall.

Fran's heart was thumping. The hurried exit from the crowd... his not answering about Thanksgiving... the reclusion into her room for dinner rather than the bantering with the count in the kitchen which Walter always enjoyed, and his saying the little cedar chest was for memories not hopes—all that was whirling turbulently in her mind.

Fran saw herself, a child of five or six, being left at camp for the first time, her parents departing. She had been so terrified that fear had stopped the words in her mouth. She wanted to cry out, Stop, don't leave me here, but couldn't. That's what she felt with Walter and again she could express nothing.

"I wish I didn't have to tell you," he was saying. "I wish I could have written it, but I couldn't. I tried not to come this time, but it was impossible not to be with you. You see, there is not going to be another time for us—no Thanksgiving, nothing else."

Fran couldn't reach those words, held ready someplace in her consciousness: Yes, I've always known, I've been waiting. She looked stunned but quiet. Walter took her hands quickly in his, rubbing them warm. She continued to sit motionless, her eyes still focused far away on the view towards Assisi. Where was her patron saint now, she asked herself nonsensically, and who would stop the wolf? Docile Umbria looked like a fake—too sweet, unreal, a perversion of the crudities actual life posed.

"We knew, didn't we," he said, "that it would have to end between us someday."

"End between us," she managed to whisper, echoing him. Yes, she nodded. Yes, she had known, that there was no alternative for them except to love and then give it up. She had tried to prepare, thinking in parables about the seven fat years and then seven lean ones; or the prudent ants vs. the feckless grasshoppers who fiddled away their summer. But none of it connected.

"Why?" she cried out, "Why? Aren't we all right as we are for a while longer? I won't stay forever. What has happened?"

"Believe me, I never wanted this to stop in this way. I would have preferred one day your leaving to go back to America. I have never wanted to hurt you."

"And now you do?"

"Christ, no!" His face was flushed now, and there was a fury in his eyes, as if he were goaded by something he couldn't fight against.

"Then why?" she cried out and her eyes filled with tears.

"Something has happened. Lucia is pregnant. For the six years of our marriage she has wanted a child but something always went wrong and she was told it might be impossible for her ever to bear children. Now she is past her third month and it looks as if she can go through with it if she stays quiet and calm. Already she is beginning to wonder about so many trips back to the field station. She could easily find out from people at the Ministry that there are no such field trips scheduled. I can't do this to her. If I upset her now, it could ruin her life. And there is the possibility of my moving from the Ministry into a better position at FAO—everything coming at once."

Walter lit a cigarette and exhaled heavily. He sat silently looking out at the country. "I couldn't write this to you -I came this last time because I had to see you once more. I won't be back."

He looked searchingly at her a long while. "You can help. Don't write to me, don't come to my office in Rome. I know it looks hard now—it looks like hell—but to do it neatly, in one blow, is best. Later you will see."

A surgeon, he was a surgeon severing neatly with one sharp incision what had become part of them both. She heard a mocking voice within her say, And now he is for the ages. And she heard the professor say, You are wrong my dear about Cassius—his wife still pleases him in bed. In fact, she was pregnant.

She said, "You say this so clinically. You've thought things out so well! You will have your wife, you will have your child—even FAO! But what of me? I will have nothing!"

"Don't say you have nothing. You will always have me as long as you care to remember. We have known something between us. Who can take that away? We were lucky to have had it—do you think it happens to everyone? And you have life—that is what is important, after all."

So, he would leave her remembrance. And she saw Dante's Francesca, speaking from the whirlwind of passion which coursed her through hell saying, There is no greater pain than in misery to recall a happy time.... So much for remembrance.

A huge fatigue settled upon her. The fatigue of endings. Calmly she said. "And you are leaving soon? Which train?"

He looked at his watch. "Let's start walking towards the station. We can go slowly."

They had to traverse a part of town that was in festive commotion, and were jostled by laughing, pushing people. Fran laughed within at the irony: it was the Day of the Dead and something had truly died that day; and no matter how sure you are of its coming, what preparations you've made to be ready, death is monstrous.

One part of her was numb, the other started planning: I will stay on in Perugia to get my certificate of proficiency in Italian from the University. I will write a farewell article to tell my readers I'm leaving. I will write to Mr. di Tomasi and tell him I'm coming back and somewhere—maybe New York—I'll try to get a job with an Italian paper. I will send Bunny a postcard addressing it to Bunny Marchi and tell her I've been in Italy over a year and have never seen a Wop. I will walk a last few times to Porta Sole and the olive groves. I will go out of Umbria as I came, alone. There'll be a rosy glow to Umbria when the bus leaves in late afternoon. The rocks will be rosy, the hills bathed in rosy light, and every so often there'll be a pink farmhouse among the silver-green olive trees. I'll drop it all into my memory chest. I'll take a ship from Naples—no crossing the Alps in the other direction -and be back for Christmas. That's it.

At the station people were pouring in from the country to join the festa. Only Walter seemed to be leaving. He stayed on the platform with her when his train pulled in. "I'm sorry for you," he said, "and I'm sorry for me. But it is the best thing to let go now. It would be harder, the more we went on. In a while it will hurt less... with time we can look back and remember the happy part."

Again he says, remember. Too late to take a snapshot of him to put in the little chest. Fran looked at him with tears in her eyes, her voice husky. "It's like saying goodbye to a part of myself. When you go in that train, part of me will be gone forever."

"And the part that stays will truly be you, stronger than before."

The train whistle blew.

That was the way Walter would go. There would be no clap of thunder, no crash. Only a train whistle and then a distant clack of wheels on track. Life and the Feast of the Dead would go on. This is the way the world ends, said the poet, not with a bang but a whimper. She echoed, this is the way love ends.

He kissed her gently over her face. He swung onto the train. From a compartment he lowered a window and leaned out towards her. "Good luck to you," he called, "I really mean it." The train began to move.

Now she laughed. His words struck her as really funny. She waved. She called, *Auguri e figli maschi!* The train gathered speed. Frantically she thought, what can I keep? Nothing again would ever be clear because she had learned that involvement is always a blur, never neatly arranged despite orderly minds and their systems. The knowledge helped her. She could believe in such a chiaroscuro world, in a life that was continual passage between shadings.

Beginnings deceive, she thought; they seem so clear—as in, just cross the Alps into the promised land. And perhaps there is no end, just a going on until we fade from view like a train departing the station.

His face at the window began to recede but she thought she could still see his stretched-out hand even as the train went out of sight. She listened hard, hearing the clackety-clack in the approaching twilight, standing there still until she could hear nothing more.

About the Author

Helen Barolini's fiction and non-fiction has created a bridge between the United States, her homeland, and Italy, her ancestral land. Awarded a writing grant from the National Endowment for the Arts for her first novel, *Umbertina* (1979), Barolini is the author of nine other books and many short stories and essays that have been cited in annual editions of *Best of American Essays*. She is also the editor of the historic anthology *The Dream Book. An Anthology of Writings by Italian American Women* (1986, 2000).

She has received an American Book Award and other honors, has been a Resident Fellow at the Rockefeller Foundation's Bellagio Center on Lake Como, and a visiting artist at the American Academy in Rome. Three of her books have appeared in translation in Italy where she has lectured as an invited American author. In 2007 she spoke on her late husband, Antonio Barolini, at a conference in Padua, Italy.

Given the intercultural themes of her work linking her American birth and education with her ancestral Italy, Helen Barolini has participated in international conferences and her work has been the subject of many student theses both here and abroad.

She has also been honored by MELUS, the American Italian Cultural Roundtable, the Sons of Italy, the Italian Welfare League, and other organizations for her literary work on the Italian American experience.

VIA FOLIOS

A refereed book series dedicated to Italian studies and the culture of Italian Americans in North America.

Published by BORDIGHERA, INC., an independently owned not-for-profit scholarly organization that has no legal affiliation to the University of Central Florida or the John D. Calandra Italian American Institute, Queens College, City University of New York.

GARDAPHÉ, GIORDANO, AND TAMBURRI
Introducing Italian Americana: Generalities
on Literature and Film
Vol. 40, Criticism $10.00

DANIELA GIOSEFFI
Blood Autumn/Autunno di sangue
Vol. 39, Poetry, $15.00/$25.00

FRED MISURELLA
Lies to Live by
Vol. 38, Stories, $15.00

STEVEN BELLUSCIO
Constructing a Bibliography
Vol. 37, Italian Americana, $15.00

ANTHONY JULIAN TAMBURRI, ED.
Italian Cultural Studies 2002
Vol. 36, Essays, $18.00

BEA TUSIANI
con amore
Vol. 35, Memoir, $19.00

FLAVIA BRIZIO-SKOV, ED.
Reconstructing Societies in the
Aftermath of War
Vol. 34, History/Cultural Studies, $30.00

ANTHONY JULIAN TAMBURRI et al
Italian Cultural Studies 2001
Vol. 33, Essays, $18.00

ELIZABETH GIOVANNAMESSINA, ED.
In Our Own Voices
Vol. 32, Ital. Amer. Studies, $25.00

STANISLAO G. PUGLIESE
Desperate Inscriptions
Vol. 31, History, $12.00

HOSTERT & TAMBURRI, EDS.
Screening Ethnicity
Vol. 30, Ital. Amer. Culture, $25.00

G. PARATI & B. LAWTON, EDS.
Italian Cultural Studies
Vol. 29, Essays, $18.00

HELEN BAROLINI
More Italian Hours & Other Stories
Vol. 28, Fiction, $16.00

FRANCO NASI, ed.
Intorno alla Via Emilia
Vol. 27, Culture, $16.00

ARTHUR L. CLEMENTS
The Book of Madness and Love
Vol. 26, Poetry, $10.00

JOHN CASEY, ET AL.
Imagining Humanity
Vol. 25, Interdisciplinary Studies, $18.00

ROBERT LIMA
Sardinia • Sardegna
Vol. 24, Poetry, $10.00

DANIELA GIOSEFFI
Going On
Vol. 23, Poetry, $10.00

ROSS TALARICO
The Journey Home
Vol. 22, Poetry, $12.00

EMANUEL diPASQUALE
The Silver Lake Love Poems
Vol. 21, Poetry, $7.00

JOSEPH TUSIANI
Ethnicity
Vol. 20, Selected Poetry, $12.00

JENNIFER LAGIER
Second Class Citizen
Vol. 19, Poetry, $8.00

FELIX STEFANILE
The Country of Absence
Vol. 18, Poetry, $9.00

PHILIP CANNISTRARO
Blackshirts
Vol. 17, History, $12.00

LUIGI RUSTICHELLI, ED.
Seminario sul racconto
Vol. 16, Narrativa, $10.00

Breinigsville, PA USA
08 December 2010
250853BV00002B/7/P